Haydn Middleton was born in Reading and studied History at Oxford, where he now lives. He has worked in advertising and publishing, lectured in British myth and legend, and written a dozen works of fiction and non-fiction.

'Haydn Middleton has successfully captured the mystery as well as the brutal tragedy of the Arthurian story. What makes *The Mordred Cycle* so powerful is the underlying weight of sexuality and universal myth which pervades it. There's a great new story being told – you have no sense what the outcome will be. And that, perhaps, is the best recommendation of all for reading these books'
Michael Moorcock

'The story of Mordred feels as if Haydn Middleton has hacked it with the strong blows of a primitive axe, instead of written it. He has hewn out of the violence of British history a terrible and disturbing legend'
Sara Banerji

'Middleton combines a poet's feel for language with a startlingly original insight into what myths actually mean: above all, he understands that the best use for a tradition is as a beach-head for innovation'
Tom Holt

'Haydn Middleton has tunnelled deep into the myth of Arthur . . . to explore its sexual and psychological underworld. He has emerged with a dark, brooding, visceral vision (that looks back to Oedipus and Electra and forward to Freud) and adds strange, powerful layers of new meaning and mystery to the legend'
Tim Pears

THE QUEEN'S CAPTIVE

A
Mordred Cycle
Novel

HAYDN MIDDLETON

WARNER BOOKS

A *Warner* Book

First published in Great Britain by Little, Brown 1996
This edition published by Warner Books 1997

Copyright © Haydn Middleton 1996

The moral right of the author has been asserted.

A CIP catalogue record for this book
is available from the British Library.

ISBN 0 7515 1661 9

Typeset in Bembo by
Palimpsest Book Production Limited,
Polmont, Stirlingshire
Printed and bound in Great Britain by
Clays Ltd, St Ives plc

UK companies, institutions and other organisations wishing
to make bulk purchases of this or any other book
published by Little, Brown should contact their local
bookshop or the special sales department at the address below.
Tel 0171 911 8000. Fax 0171 911 8100.

Warner Books
A Division of
Little, Brown and Company (UK)
Brettenham House
Lancaster Place
London WC2E 7EN

The first name that this island bore, when it was held by the giants and then saved by Arthur from the Sea Wolves: Albion.

And after Arthur fell in the deluge, the rump that remained was called Avalon. And when Arthur returned, it rose again and became Logres.

And the blood of one man ran through all these kingdoms. His name was Mordred . . .

PROLOGUE

The barge moved fast though he felt no wind. Fast through the dark with his eyes shut tight. His skin was stained, his hair damply matted. The blade of his knife was still warm from its work. King's blood, dream blood, spilled to kill a kingdom. He opened his mouth to defend what he had done. The women closed in with their tongues and their fingers:

'Sleep now, don't tell us. Just sleep until Avalon . . .'

He wanted to sleep. He wanted it badly. Sleep as a cage for the dream he had butchered. Nothing, he knew, now remained from before. But nothing had risen yet out of its ruins. No other place he could go to be free.

Tighter he curled himself, small in the current. 'Sleep,' sang the women, all seven in unison. 'Sleep to reach Avalon, take yourself there . . .'

The barge now was hurtling. They prised the knife from him, then pulled at his tunic until it was gone. Their hands were all over him, gentle and expert. He liked their attention:

his seven new mothers. He wanted to please them, to be what they needed.

Their touch was so subtle, like waves washing over him. Women or water, he no longer knew. He smiled in his dark sleep with no barge beneath him. Drowning bone-dry as the current rushed on. Beautiful sleep after such a great bloodletting. No speaking, no saying, no need to explain.

He wanted to stay there, among them and naked. But a new hand was closing now, drawing him upward. He screamed and no sound came; he woke and drowned deeper. The hand gripped him harder, the darkness grew larger.

'Where are you taking me?' pulsed through his body.

'Closer to Logres . . .' A voice soft and fluid – the voice of a woman he half-thought he knew. 'Logres is waiting, we'll find it through you . . .'

The hand hauled him higher. It broke his own surface, then set him afloat on a new kind of earth.

Part One

EARTH

ONE

The girl came at sunset. It had to be the girl. None of the older women had been up from the shore in all the twenty days since Morgan had arrived.

'Join me,' Morgan beckoned. Sitting up straighter, she patted the slab of marble which surrounded the fountain in the villa's central courtyard. At her feet lay the debris of the meal she was still eating: a barely touched basket of mussels, some olive stones and fishbones, a few half-eaten figs. All of it had been set out earlier by the girl. All would be cleared up by her after. But she came no closer now, and she looked at Morgan oddly, warily, as if she didn't quite dare to speak.

'What is it?' Morgan asked. 'Tell me.'

The girl's eyes widened. Night-blue eyes over a tiny tilted nose. Sometimes Morgan thought the mysterious women sent her up as a tease — as if to say: here, the only one of us who will speak to you is the one who can tell you the least.

But then the girl glanced behind her, along the colonnade towards the top of the cliff-path up which she had come running. 'Down there,' she said at last in her cautious, possibly slow-witted way. 'You should come and see.'

'See what?' Morgan pulled the wrap tighter around her shoulders. Wherever this place was, its climate was one of striking extremes. The evenings could be as sharp as the days were all so beautifully warm.

'A man. A new man.'

Suddenly she dropped to the ground and fanned out her limbs. 'He is stretched like this,' she called up. Then she raised her knees and turned them to the side. 'No. Like this.'

Morgan grinned and the girl got up. Primly she slapped at her ragged blue shift to beat out the dust. She smiled so seldom, and even then it always seemed to be against her better judgement. Her name was Anna; she was eight years old, with a mess of squirrel-red hair and a pretty oval face that was filthy with freckles.

'Why do you want me to come and see this man?' asked Morgan. 'I mean, why this one? I know there have been others. I've seen them from the cliff top.'

She had only seen anything from the cliff top; she hadn't yet felt the need to go any closer. For the twenty days of her recuperation, since dragging herself ashore and up the cliff-path, she had been more than happy to live in parallel with the women. They had their own solemn world down there at the water's edge; she had hers up here. She had no idea who they were or what their real

6

business was. For all she knew, they too had been on the boat that had brought her into this exile, and now they were keeping her under a loose kind of surveillance.

'Tell me why you want me to see this man,' she repeated.

The girl grabbed a hank of hair and fed its ends into the side of her mouth. 'He is not like the others.'

Morgan breathed in. In spite of herself she pictured a great dark cross arising from the sea. Muscular, regal, amphibian. . . Automatically her right hand moved under her wrap to touch the golden band that circled her left upper arm. 'In what way not like the others?'

'They were all Land Men.'

'Land Men?' Morgan gripped her armlet tighter.

Anna nodded, as if what she had said were self-evident. 'And this one is alive. He is breathing. So they can't put him into the land.'

She glanced all around her, at the fountain, the pool, the stag-and-hunter mosaic under Morgan's bare feet. It was always so hard to hold her attention and, in her own infant way, she could seem as forbidding as the women.

The first time they had spoken, Morgan had asked which of them was her mother. The girl had just laughed. 'There was danger, so we came here,' was all she said when Morgan had pressed her again. Now she gnawed on her hair, rocking on the heel of one foot. *They can't put him into the land . . .*

Morgan felt nervous but unsurprised. The dead men on the shore had all been of a horribly familiar kind. To Anna they might have been 'Land Men'. To Morgan

7

they were Arthur's Men – otherwise known as strays or merlins – and all of them were messengers from her own private hell. It intrigued her that so many merlins should have fetched up here dead. What new crisis could have hit the land she had been driven from? But she had guessed that in the end one of them would get through alive, with news for her or even orders.

'This new man,' she said, standing and pulling the wrap so taut at her neck that it chafed, 'has he asked to see me?'

'No.' Anna shrugged, looking hard at Morgan as if she might be about to ask or suggest something much more exciting. Then she glanced up. 'Look!' she cried, pointing above Morgan's head at one of the male statues that watched over the courtyard. A cormorant – as black as Morgan's hair – had winged in to perch on its dazzling white shoulder. 'It's trying to eat his eyes!'

The bird did appear to be pecking at the blank marble sockets. Then it flew off, leaving an olive-coloured squirt dripping down the statue's side.

Morgan's left hand rose to the flat of her stomach. The girl followed the movement curiously. 'The women then,' Morgan continued, 'did they tell you to come and fetch me?'

The girl tilted her head and after a moment's thought nodded.

'You want me to come now?' Morgan asked. 'With you?'

Anna nodded again, then turned and sped away.

Morgan followed at her own steady pace, but without

first pausing to slip into her sandals. Walking was still a little difficult for her, even though the scars had quickly healed since her arrival and most of the bruising had disappeared.

The dark was closing in fast. Already the smoke from the women's night torches was acrid on the air. Late silent seagulls arrowed overhead, making for the nearer of the two headlands that formed the wide bay.

Anna had told her that the whole place was an island. 'Avalon', she had called it. Morgan had never heard the name before. She thought it might even have been a child's way of saying 'Albion', an archaic term for the kingdom of Arthur that she had come from. Morgan presumed that this was in fact one of that kingdom's adjacent isles. One of the many. An enlightened kind of penal colony perhaps? After all, the voyage had been very short. Far too short for Morgan to have travelled beyond the range of Arthur's authority.

The path down the cliff was even steeper than she remembered. Twice she lost her footing and had to twist around to grab at dry tussocks. The second time, she grazed one of her still-tender breasts and gasped.

Anna drew farther ahead, falling once herself and then skipping on faster. She jumped down into the scrub, ran headlong past the cairns that marked the dead men's graves, and finally on to the sand.

The women were waiting in a torchlit crescent with their backs to the receding tide. Seven women. Always seven, but not – it had seemed to Morgan from on high – always the same women. A dark shape lay to their right: a man's shape but, unlike all the stilled, leather-clad bodies that Morgan had glimpsed before, this one was naked.

For the briefest moment she was stirred. It was almost as if she had recognized him, even from so far away. Just a merlin ... she reminded herself. Just another merlin ...

Down on the strand it was warmer than above. The air seemed barely to be circulating. Carefully Morgan picked her way around the cairns and over the scatters of pebble. The smoother sand was springy from the tide. Feeling the water bubble up between her toes again, she remembered how confusing her own arrival had been. She had woken alone in the becalmed and empty boat, still drugged and damaged from what had gone before. Water had always frightened her, but she had had to wade painfully ashore, waist deep at first, praying she would not fall and go under.

Twenty days had passed since then, though it felt like twenty years. Twenty good years. Time moved so languidly here. Each moment seemed determined not to give way to the next. But it moved so sweetly too, somehow restoring her as it went, coaxing her to rise up through the ruins of herself. Slowly but surely, and entirely unexpectedly, she had come to think that she was being given a second chance. But now there was this man.

She kept her eyes on his shape up ahead. On the mass of dark, tangled hair – the surest sign of a merlin. She approached at an angle so that she could see the whole curled length of him.

Once, in the wartime, the merlins had been little more than bits of breath twisted into bone and skin. Not so much men as messages made flesh – and the messages for Morgan had always been bad. Now the merlins came in many shapes and sizes. Leathery, lizardy, doglike too. In this one's posture there was something at least semi-human, as if he had just rolled over on to his side after making love. Again Morgan felt that pang of familiarity.

But the closer she came, the smaller he seemed to grow. It was more than just a trick of the fast-fading light. At times, when off her guard, Morgan could see far deeper than she ever wanted to. He seemed to be shrinking in years as well as in size. By the time she was within reach of his feet, he could have been a foetus: swimming towards her powerfully fast, laughing through sharp teeth, brandishing fists, a blade, a new king's black flesh cross . . .

A stab of pain made Morgan double up. It was as if she had been kicked inside her stomach.

Slowly she straightened, afraid that she might vomit. From the corner of her eye she saw Anna step out towards her. She waved her back, then smiled. They came and went, these pains: echoes of the pregnancy. She didn't resent them in the way that she resented and feared her intermittent visions. They helped her to think that the child hadn't truly left her behind for ever.

She looked down and saw the new merlin as he really was.

He was young, younger than herself, probably not

yet twenty. Anna had mimed his position well. Arms spread, knees raised, heavily bearded face averted. He looked as if he had been crucified down there – pinned to the sand through his feet and uncalloused palms. And although his dry skin was pale his body hair was startlingly dark. A great swatch spilled from the crown of his head, merging with the pelt that coated his torso and slender limbs, curling into tough-looking tendrils at his groin. *Not like the others. . .*

Morgan raised her eyes. The tide slunk back uncertain in the smoky dark, like a dog that had dumped a smaller half-savaged beast at its master's feet.

She turned to look at the women.

This was the nearest she had ever come to them. From a distance they had sometimes looked ghostly with their milky skins and silver-blonde hair and gossamer dresses. Closer to, they seemed hardly more substantial. And whether or not they were her guards, they had to be working to some kind of rota. Usually they were all around Morgan's own age, certainly well under thirty, but that evening two looked twice as old. Four carried pitch torches, the heat of which made each of them shimmer as if they were under water. Farther up the shore a brazier was sending out more billows.

Each of the seven met her gaze levelly. Wryly, almost. As if to show that they had heard all the merlins' tales about Morgan's eyes and found them only amusing. Their faces were handsome but gave nothing away.

'So,' Morgan smiled, too nervous to keep a cynical

edge out of her voice, 'are you now going to tell me what I'm meant to be doing here?'

None of them answered, but Morgan knew that they must have heard because Anna twisted her head and looked up at them expectantly.

'You wanted me down here,' she called into the stillness. 'Why did you want me to see him?' She waved at the body with a hand that she then placed on her stomach. Again she smiled. 'Have you been told not to speak to me?'

She narrowed her eyes at them. In that poor evening light and the heat and the gentle breeze, they seemed to ripple together like an upright rock-pool. It was possible, she supposed, that they didn't speak her language. She had never heard them speaking to one another in any tongue.

'What do you want me to do?' she asked. 'Why am I here? And what's so special about this man?'

'He's alive,' Anna piped up, as if that explained everything. Then she added: 'He should be in the house.'

Morgan nodded slowly. Seven sets of sea-green eyes made no response. There was nothing to debate; no way of debating it. Morgan pulled her wrap so tightly around herself that she heard some threads tear. It crossed her mind, ludicrously, that they were wanting her to carry him up herself.

She gazed back inland. To the cliff, the diagonal path, the red-tiled roof of the villa that she had taken for her own luxurious home from home. She had felt like a queen inside it, but now there was going to be a king as well. For all she knew it really was a sanatorium, for anyone who needed it. She had dearly hoped that she was being given a second chance here, and maybe that was still the truth. But a second chance for what?

Her eyes fell to the graves: the cairns that clustered in the high cliff's shadow. A little man-garden; the corpses planted out like seed. And here at her feet this looked like the garden's first fruit, a genuine 'Land Man'.

'Yes, then,' she called over her shoulder as she turned and set off back towards the cliff-path. 'Bring him up.'

The villa was different with the women inside it. Morgan had previously seen it as her castle. Now she felt less secure, even though they looked to her for gestured directions and seemed not to know their own way around.

She didn't want the stranger in her own quarters, so she led his carriers to the bath-house across the courtyard. There she prepared a couch near the big pool. She also lit the brazier, less to warm the room than to raise some smoke against the new man's own subtle aura. Finally she laid out the most suitable clothing she could find – a simple black hooded cloak – bowls for water to clean him, and also a ewer of wine and some cups.

None of the women would drink with her. Morgan took several mouthfuls of the sour liquor anyway. It gave her the courage to ask them, as they then made to leave, if they would wash and clothe him. When they looked back blankly, she mimed both actions. At once they went to fill the bowls with pool water.

Morgan watched from the arch that gave on to the vine-heavy colonnade. 'Is it strange to touch someone living,' she asked softly as they began, twisting an unbound strand of her long jet hair around her finger. 'After all of your corpses down there?'

She expected and got no answer. No one even looked up from the couch, the bowls, and the sodden rags ripped from a single silken sheet.

Leaning against the architrave, Morgan shifted her weight from one foot to the other. Grains of wet sand from the shore clung to her soles. She wished little Anna had come up too, and wondered why she had been left behind. It crossed her mind that something might be about to happen which a child shouldn't have to see.

Still holding her wine-cup, she stepped gingerly into the room and, taking a rushlight from the brazier, reached up to set the lanterns on each wall burning. She kept snatching glances at the seven as she circled the pool. Their dresses were ragged, stained and, near the hems of several, almost certainly blood-spattered. Quickly she returned to the arch.

'Have there been no others?' Morgan asked. 'Survivors?'

She imagined that there hadn't been. The women's handling of this one looked so unpractised. They grabbed and turned him as if they were priming a set of chops. And survivors of *what*? Morgan wondered again.

Clumsily the women shuffled him into the long garment. Seven women; fourteen hands. Morgan thought of all the dead men they had touched, all the death that had passed through their fingers. As the lower part of his body was at last hidden from her sight, she felt dizzy with relief.

The seven stepped back, forming another crescent under the rushlight. Morgan felt overawed by them, yet they seemed to be awaiting dismissal. Nothing was the right way round here. Morgan, in banishment, held a form of authority. She had come ashore expecting to be watched over at every turn, yet now – it seemed – she was expected to watch over someone else.

She stared at him. Under this roof he unnerved her more than out on the sand. His blue-black mane was splayed out over the head of the couch. He seemed to be drowning where he lay. Drowning on dry land. If she were left alone with him now, she was afraid that she might be dragged in too. She didn't know what could be wrong with him, but he would need so much attention. So much patient care. It would be like looking after a child.

Closing her eyes, she took a deep breath. 'Why won't you tell me what to do?' she asked through gritted teeth. 'Why does it have to be like this? Can't you explain to me where I am, and what I'm meant to do here?'

Morgan glared then at each silent woman in turn. Tears welled at the corners of her eyes. 'Couldn't you stay?' she asked a little more shrilly. 'Now that you've come inside? You don't have to sleep down there on the shore.' She took another mouthful of the wine which had already gone to her head. 'I just don't know what to do with him!'

She smiled, trying to recover herself, but the women had already lowered their eyes. 'Do you know who I am?' she breathed, her wet eyes blazing. This wasn't just an attempt to assert herself. Back in the kingdom, thanks largely to the slurs cast by the merlins, most people outside the court had known her for what she was, not who. It was still just possible that whoever these eerie women were, they hadn't been told a thing about her.

They looked back unabashed, simply needing her permission to leave. But Morgan needed more. She took a deeper breath.

'Arthur . . .' she murmured, wincing with the effort of saying his name. 'You know of *him*? You know who Arthur is . . . ?'

A breeze seemed to pass through the seven, rustling them into a quietly defiant show of life. The woman nearest to Morgan raised her right hand, and for a moment Morgan thought she was going to cross herself. That would have been bizarre enough. But then the woman startled her even more by extending her forefinger and drawing it almost seductively across her throat.

Morgan chuckled. 'Arthur? *Dead*?'

The woman let her hand fall but held Morgan in her gaze. The six others were watching her too. Morgan looked from one to another, her grin fixed. Maybe there was just a little sympathy in their eyes now. She put her head to one side, and slid her right hand under her wrap to touch the armlet that she had never, even here, dared to take off.

'The king?' she checked, in case they meant some

other Arthur. She was shivering, gripping her wine-cup so tightly that its bronze rim buckled. 'How could he be dead?'

None of them responded. Morgan wondered if she really had seen the woman's finger pass across her throat. She put the cup to her lips again and drained it. Then she bent to set it down on the ground next to the ewer, bracing herself in anticipation of a pain that didn't slice through her. She saw nothing but the black cross rising, just the mark and not the man: grisly, deathless, always out of water. Straightening, she placed a hand on her stomach.

'The king must be alive,' she said in a low, flat voice.

The words had found their own way out. They could have been spewed up from the pool, or even from the mouth of the man on his couch. But she knew that what she had said was true. Arthur was alive. Whatever new war had erupted in his kingdom, whyever all these corpses kept on littering this shore – in any way that mattered, Arthur himself couldn't die. Least of all for Morgan.

The women watched as if she were performing on a stage, and they were a paying audience. But they were the actresses here, they the entertainers.

'Oh, go,' Morgan said, stepping aside so that they could file past. 'Leave the bowls and rags. Leave it all . . .'

When the last had left the room she pressed her back against the arch and stared hard at her new charge. 'You will have everything you need,' Guenever had promised Morgan before she had been bundled off to the waiting boat. 'You'll be safer, and you will have everything you need . . .'

Morgan's heart heaved, her legs felt hollow. As so often on this island, she had the sensation that she was floating – in water, not in air. That her feet hadn't been on solid ground since the moment she had climbed down from the boat.

A man. A new man . . . A 'Land Man' surely, even if he looked less and less like all the others. Morgan needed him to be a merlin. It was so much easier to resent him if he was. Slowly she closed her eyes.

Once the merlins had been so vital, the sole links between one war-torn quarter of Arthur's kingdom and another. Bringing news first of disasters as the incoming Sea Wolves swept all before them, then of triumphs as Arthur made the tide turn. But in Arthur's so-called Age of Gold, any man could travel the kingdom's length without a hair on his head being harmed. There was nothing more for the merlins to say. No more chaos for them to shape, save as simple storytellers, re-heating the war's horrors for men who still needed that. Or forging semi-fictions from the peace. 'A seed sown in darkness,' they had whispered about Morgan herself, 'will surely blossom in an evil way.' They had vilified her just as unfairly as they had glorified Arthur. So she felt no pity now if they were dying in droves.

New footsteps sounded behind her in the colonnade, but Morgan was still too preoccupied even to turn her head.

Anna skipped past, scooping up the wine cup as she

went. She dipped it into the pool, then knelt next to the couch. Morgan absently wondered whether she had come of her own accord or if the women had sent her.

'You will not have to do this part,' the little girl announced over her shoulder. 'I can look after him. I can do it well.'

Immediately she reached out, cradled the sleeper's head in the crook of her small arm, and started to slip some of the water between his lips. She clucked encouragements as if she were playing with a doll or a pet. Morgan couldn't see his throat move, but not a drop spilled down.

Anna turned again, holding up the inverted cup to show that it was empty. 'See,' she said. 'I told you I can do this part of it.'

This part. Morgan stared at her, surprised first of all to see that the girl was quite serious, and then to find that she was nodding her own head in acceptance.

TWO

The arrangement held for a week.

Every afternoon Anna arrived punctually to do her new job. Morgan wasn't proud to be letting the little girl feed, clean and occasionally re-clothe a grown man. She insisted at least on making a thin gruel for him each morning and setting it down next to the pool. But while the child was then visiting, she kept herself well out of the way.

Often she withdrew to her bed, endlessly combing and dressing her sumptuous hair in front of the long mirror. She was pleased with the reflections this mirror gave her. Tall and willowy though she was, it made her seem taller and even more svelte. Her high cheekbones looked even higher, her lips a little more generous, her skin more golden than tawny. And then there were her eyes. Less deep, less wide, less lustrous than she'd ever seen them – and thus less likely to breed crass rumours. Demon's eyes, the merlins had called them before. The eyes of an aberrant Fay. Her stare, they said, could split rocks, scorch trees and spellbind any man. But not here. Not any more.

During other visits from Anna she went to one of the outbuildings, to weave badly on an old loom she had uncovered earlier. At other times again she sat for hours in the breezy sunlight by the fountain, or tried to lose herself in the rose gardens and vineyards.

One afternoon she wandered right through the sprawling apple orchards behind the villa. The grass here was browner, the trees less carefully spaced. From the villa's rear gateway she liked to look out on this gently rising hinterland, its skyline always blurred by the heat or the rain. The sense of infinity pleased her. She saw herself poised at the thin end of a wedge that shelved up all the way up to Christ's heaven.

After walking for two hours she stopped, sat, and gazed back seawards, holding up her hair behind to let the breeze play on her neck. The one-storied villa shone white like a squared-off seashell over the bay.

Even from here, the whole lush estate had a calming effect. The deep, restorative quiet was only ever broken by bird cries or the regular swirling rain showers. Not the enforced kind of hush that Morgan had once known in the kingdom's chapels or monasteries. Speech here surely wouldn't have been forbidden, but the atmosphere seemed to be inviting other, subtler ways of making contact. With herself more than with anyone else. And it was working. For the first time in her life, she had been happy here by herself. For the first time ever, she had liked to be alone.

From this elevation, the villa's enclosure wall looked higher than she had imagined. She could only just see inside to the various blocks of rooms arranged around the fountain courtyard. She presumed that the ancient giants had built it, but it was much better preserved than their works in the kingdom. It seemed, in fact, to have been continuously occupied, with its well-appointed gardens and spare, pastel furnishings.

She had never expected to find such a haven – in spite of Guenever's promise at her frantic departure. This little world had fitted itself around her like the surface of a lake around a new lily. But nothing was simple. In spite of her relief and gratitude, she had never been blind to the oddness around her. She had been exiled from the kingdom in early May, yet after only hours at sea she had come ashore here in high summer.

Morgan could recall almost nothing about the voyage now. In far too much pain to take notice of what was happening around her, she couldn't remember the face of a single crewman now. She had wept and moaned and then slept; and when she awoke she had been on her own, marooned off this shore.

At first she had thought the land was a mirage, even after setting foot on it and settling into the empty villa: a lovely, soft dream that was sure not to last. But nothing had changed. It was as if she had crossed bodily into a new and better world. Not an afterworld, exactly; more like an alternative to any world she knew. Since the first day, the

23

past had seemed to be falling away more quickly than the future came on; stripping her of her old dependent self, making her see how to thrive on her own. A process of some kind was surely under way. That, presumably, was why she was here. And now the newcomer was a part of it. The new sleeping lord.

His presence had made such a difference. Somehow he seemed to suit the villa better than Morgan did. Maybe, like a fickle cat, the place inclined itself to whoever came into it last.

But for all Morgan knew, it really was his own, and the women had simply brought him back to his home. Maybe all the merlins had come from here. They must have come from somewhere. And finally, when there were no more tales to tell, they had to have somewhere to go back to.

On returning late that evening, she lay awake for hours. When she'd had the villa to herself her sleep had been deep and dreamless. Since sharing it, she had had very little rest at all. The new man seemed to have filled the place. The musky, fishy stink of him; the silent roar of the rhythm of his sleep. Whenever Morgan closed her eyes she saw his body-hair spreading like ivy around the pool, up the fluted pillars that supported its roof.

The sea, too, seemed noisier since his coming. More insistent. At times its tidal crash and hiss almost sounded like words. Or just one word, over and over. A word that sounded like 'con-fess'.

She rose at dawn after the shallowest sleep, having dreamed repeatedly of the sea; not just scouring the shore now but seeping up over the cliff, lapping at the enclosure wall, threatening to sweep the villa away. She paced her room in the fading dark, watching her own slim shape gather in the mirror. As she did so, another dream from her troubled sleep surfaced.

She had been standing at some vessel's prow, backed by the women, trawling dark waters off a bleaker shore than this, and had looked down to see that she was wearing a bloodied silken birthing-robe. A figure was wading out towards her, reaching up through the mists, wanting to be brought on board. She thought at first that it was a child. But as he came closer he aged and grew. Black-haired, tall and lithe, bloodstained himself. It was the sleeper, and he looked so innocent, so un-merlinlike.

When his hand came to hers, it passed clean through her flesh. Again and again. He was trying to tell her that he had killed a man, that the blood on him was not his own. 'It *is* your blood,' Morgan remembered replying without rancour, pointing to her own stains, remembering how all the merlins' lies had made her suffer. 'Your blood, mine, the king's: ours . . .'

Intrigued and oddly emboldened by the dream, she left the room in her night clothes and strode across the courtyard to where the new man lay. He hadn't shifted his position. His closed eyes were still directed at the ceiling. From a distance Morgan thought she saw small fat marks on his neck, arms and legs. Cuts maybe, leech-shaped.

She touched her throat in panic, but when she peered closer they vanished. She took a large gulp of the clotted air. It was as if a storm had recently broken around him without affecting any other part of the house. He's come with his own weather, she thought. Just the way Arthur used to. The king who couldn't die. The king who perished only in stories.

She stopped just short of the couch, her boldness gone. Again she could only steal glances; not size him up frankly. The sleeping lord and his sleepless keeper.

From where she stood, she could have reached out and touched his hand. Such a soft, unscabbed hand, dark with hair from just above the knuckle. It lay open, almost inviting her fingers in. In spite of herself, Morgan felt tempted, but she couldn't do it. Not just because he was a merlin. Her dream had been so vivid. She was also half-afraid that her hand might pass right through him . . .

Two mornings later, shortly after dawn, she wandered out to the cliff-top for the first time since the new man's arrival. Under guttering torches tied to poles planted in the sand, the seven women pored over a fresh set of corpses.

The tide was some way out and the light still dim, but Morgan saw a shape bobbing in the shallows. A masted barge perhaps, better suited to river travel. But when she looked harder she could see no vessel of any sort. It couldn't have crossed the blurred horizon or even gone under so quickly. In matters of time here, however, she was coming to expect the unexpected.

She stayed at the cliff-top till the sun broke through, swathed by the thin smoke coiling up from the torches. The low-murmuring sea still seemed to be trying to speak. It sounded all around her. She felt that she was floating on it, buoyed up by the noise, as if the whole world had turned liquid: the sand, rocks and scrub just so much painted water. And when she closed her eyes she felt that time was flying past faster than ever, but banking up behind her, maybe dangerously high.

To reorientate herself she finally let her eyes linger on the bodies. It was impossible to tell whether all the merlins had died in the water or before entering it. The women manhandled them in such a graceless silence. Sirens without a song, Morgan thought as she turned and headed back.

On returning from the orchards, much later that day, she found the villa chillier than usual. She lit the braziers in her own rooms, then went in to see the sleeper. She half-hoped that he would have risen and vanished like Christ on the third day. But still he was there. More troublingly, the bowls that Morgan had laid out that morning for Anna hadn't been touched.

She went closer to him. He lay flat on his back, arms stiff at his sides, his cushioned head turned towards the pool. Both his cloak and the couch were clean. His smell from here was neither musky nor fishy but faintly smoky, as if Anna hadn't yet scrubbed away the full taint of the women's torches.

He looked older than before – as if he had been putting on years as he lay there, gently accumulating age until he reached the point where he could wake and be himself. Morgan chewed her lip. She was no wiser to him than she had been on his arrival. Maybe he was still slowly arriving, the shell of his body having been sent on ahead to receive his soul and senses later.

Taking a taper from the brazier's untended embers, she lit the lanterns. She felt he was watching her pace barefoot round the pool – and she couldn't make herself look back to check that his eyes were closed. She was starting to feel that he stalked her always, both inside the villa and out. He seemed to be biding his time. Like those infants who won't speak a word for years, then suddenly start to talk in fully formed sentences.

At last she came back to him. His breathing was light but regular. Morgan knelt next to the couch, bringing her breast level with his head. Her hands felt numb and she kept her head averted, as if her breath might contaminate him. She stared at his peacock-tail display of black hair. So long, so anciently mossed and braided. Briefly she longed to reach out and stroke it. She also felt a more distant urge to knot it around his neck and strangle him.

But she couldn't hurt him. Not this one. This close, he looked almost too noble to be a merlin. There was so much more of the eagle than the lizard in his features; more of the bear than the dog. Nor could she let him die for lack of food. So, in Anna's absence, she ladled some gruel into a cup and took it around to the pool side of the couch.

She knelt again and, using the metal ladle, propped his head higher. His mouth was firmly closed, but she wouldn't touch his skin herself. It was hard enough just to look at his cracked lips and flaring nostrils. Her hands were trembling, her heart rapping against her ribs. Each

28

of his fine features sparked strong physical responses in her, but they left her feeling proud, possessive even – not, immediately, eager.

Morgan pressed the cup at him; pewter on teeth. The liquid started to course through his beard and onto the couch. She tried again, but soaked his cheek instead. Then the ladle skewed sideways under the pressure of his head, which fell back heavily. Despairing, Morgan threw down the cup.

'I'll do it,' said a small voice from the arch ahead of her.

Morgan, still kneeling, stiffened and closed her eyes. The girl couldn't have timed her entrance better. 'Were you watching?' Morgan asked, smiling at the water. 'Were you waiting there to see me make a mess of it?'

Down on her knees, with tears pricking her eyes, she felt about eight years old herself. She looked up. Anna bit on her hair, not visibly chastened. 'I am sorry I am late,' she said, but she looked more disappointed in Morgan, as if her low opinion of the older woman had now been confirmed and could never be altered. Then she skipped up to retrieve the cup. She never walked; she took everything at such a grim-faced rush.

Morgan rose and stepped aside. Soon Anna was succeeding with the merlin where Morgan herself had so signally failed. As she looked on, a sudden kick deep in her abdomen almost knocked her off balance. She staggered, wincing, and the little girl turned.

'I have seen you do that before,' she said. 'Have you got a pain?'

'No,' Morgan muttered, easing herself upright.

'What have you got, then?'

Morgan closed her eyes and shook her head. What *had* she got? Here, now? 'These Land Men, as you call them,' she said instead of answering as Anna resumed her feeding, 'do you know how they all died?'

'It was at the ending of Albion. In the deluge.' She didn't look up. She spoke flatly and fast, as if she were quoting from a lesson learned by heart.

'The *ending* of Albion?'

Anna nodded. Morgan nodded back, as if this meant something to her. 'And how did Albion end?' she asked carefully.

'In the deluge.'

'And what was the deluge?'

'The thing that ended Albion.'

Morgan smiled at the top of her head. Plainly she knew nothing; just these two empty phrases. 'But tell me,' she went on, 'have there been other Land Men like this one, down there on the shore, still alive?'

Anna looked at her nonplussed. 'This is not a Land Man. Land Men go in the ground.'

'Whatever . . . Have there been any other men down there who were living?'

'Not alive, no.' She shook her head, then paused. 'But sometimes the seven pretend that they are.'

'What do you mean?'

Anna shot a glance across the body, not quite in Morgan's direction. 'Sometimes they pretend that the men are alive. They play with them. Just for a while,

30

before they put them in the ground.' She paused again, perhaps a little too self-consciously. 'And sometimes they get them back out and do it too.'

Morgan's jaw tightened. She touched her stomach, flustered, but said nothing. There was nothing she could say – not to this child, who might in any case have been telling some innocently warped, childish version of what really went on. Instead she nodded at the sleeper.

'Don't you think he's had enough now?' she asked, ready to stand corrected.

But Anna shrugged, nodded, and laid the great black head back on its cushion. There was barely any spillage to mop up with the cuff of her ragged sleeve. When she stood, she ran her eyes up and down the couch. Morgan noticed a rare smile pucker her lips, then quickly she chewed on some hair-ends, as if to bring her mouth back under control.

'What is it?' Morgan asked. 'What's funny?'

Anna swung her upper body from side to side. 'Well, he is a man.' Her mouth twitched again. *Play with them* . . .

'Yes?' Morgan could see she was looking at his crotch. Then the girl took her breath away. As one hand still fiddled with her hair, she pushed the other into the sleeper's tunic and fondly flicked at his hidden genitals.

'Don't *do* that!' Morgan gasped, unsure in the blind moment if she were offended or envious.

Anna stood as if to attention, both arms stiff at her sides, maybe in imitation of the man. But the unaccustomed

31

smile was splitting her face, and Morgan knew that she had done all this as a deliberate challenge.

'You'd better go,' she sighed, starting to feel light-headed.

The girl went straight away, but Morgan's gaze stayed on the sleeper. She didn't know if she dared to trust her own eyes, but she was convinced that at Anna's touch she had seen him briefly stir inside his tunic.

Play . . . Her stomach lurched. Quickly she followed the girl out, leaving the crockery by the couch. By the next afternoon, after another sleepless night and morning, she had decided what to do.

She went in to find Anna beside the sleeper, sitting cross-legged and calm amid the leavings of the meal that she had already shared with him.

As Morgan entered she neither stood, smiled nor spoke. Maybe she already knew what was coming. She seemed to be looking up at Morgan like a rival. Her expression was so familiar: care-worn, reproachful, and – by some moral yardstick – superior. She could have been Guenever down there.

Morgan came closer. 'I think I'll be able to deal with him from now on,' she said. 'I think I really should. You're . . . very young.'

As if to emphasize the point, Anna grabbed a hank of her hair and bit on it.

'But thank you,' Morgan repeated, meaning that she wanted her to leave at once. Anna sprang to her feet, but made no other move to go.

'What is it?' asked Morgan. 'What are you waiting for?'

Anna met her eye. She still had her hair in her mouth. Morgan glanced from the girl's face to the man's. There *was* a rivalry between them over him, which was crazy, but it was as real as the whispering sea outside. And now he seemed to be receding beneath her, ebbing like the morning tide.

Suddenly Morgan felt driven to assert her own right and bring him back. Looking at Anna, she stepped up to the couch, reached out, and closed her hand over his.

Anna's eyes widened but she kept on chewing her hair. Morgan tightened her grip, mainly to steady herself. He was still there, her hand hadn't passed clean through him; he was as solid for her as he was for the girl. But he was cold. Savagely cold. Inside him he had to be bloodless.

His finger bones were large and smooth. Soothingly so. But the shock of touching him had tilted Morgan's own balance. She felt again as if she were floating in a waterworld, but this time clinging to him like a spar. She put a hand to her stomach, and knew from the higher damp warmth that, for the first time in weeks, milk was oozing out of her.

She ran her hand up his icy arm, against the dense hair's grain, watching the tips of her fingers disappear. She closed her eyes and the hair felt like scales; more fish than flesh beneath her. Then she looked and gripped his broad, clothed shoulder.

She wanted Anna to leave, but she needed her there too. Alone, she couldn't have come this far.

33

But the longer Anna stayed, the further she had to go.

Morgan started to knead his shoulder. Briefly she thought a muscle tensed, then yielded again. Her fingers found his bare neck, the beard that sprawled down to his collarbone. She felt the cold life in him but only faintly, as if he were breathing somewhere else and this was just its echo. She touched his throat, his chin, ran one finger between his big, bruisable lips. Her breasts felt as if they were drowning.

Yet *he* felt so dry. She pictured him purged right through: dry blood, dry spit, a desiccated husk. She wanted to slip a finger inside his mouth, just to find out that she was wrong. Instead she laid her palm flat against his cheek, his closed eye, the tangle of his eyebrow. Then she waited, entranced, like someone expecting a message to come through. Some explanation of what he was for. She was sure there had to be one.

She smiled down at his half-hidden face, wishing she could see what his eyes were like: how he would look at her, his expression when he saw her milk-stained gown. She wondered what he was called; she saw herself saying every name she knew in his ear until she spoke the right one and he woke.

Roughly she pushed her hand up into his mane, twisting it, watching a sliver of seaweed fall out on to the floor. She pulled up his head by its hair and suddenly a sound flew out of her. A sigh, sharp but shockingly sexual. It seemed to strike echoes off the pool water, while bringing Morgan's feet four-square back to the floor.

34

And it ended the contest with Anna. Wordlessly the girl turned and ran out.

As soon as she was gone Morgan, gasping, released the sleeper's head and closed her fingers over his. Again for an instant they seemed to respond to her light pressure. She pulled away as if she had been burned, then took two steps back, putting a hand to each of her leaking breasts. *Play . . .*

The room had become very cool around the two of them. Like the sleeper, it had lost all heat and colour. Morgan wrenched her gaze around to the water's calm surface.

A merlin, she struggled to tell herself again. Just another merlin. She badly wanted to drag the couch up to the pool's edge and tip him in before he had the chance to wake and be with her properly. But she knew how futile that would be. He would survive a drowning in this water just as he had survived the singing sea. He would keep on coming back.

He was hers, and now she had to have him.

THREE

It was easier than she had expected. Morgan had little trouble in meeting all the sleeper's needs. Soon she forgot why she had been so afraid.

Changing his loincloths was simple. His mess was thin, black and meagre. Cleaning him was no harder than wiping down a meal table. Feeding him came less naturally; it felt more intimate. But Morgan made herself enjoy watching the gruel slide down into him: her great, dependent cuckoo.

She became unwilling to leave his side, loath to give Anna the chance to slip back into her old role. But the girl never appeared. And still Morgan kept up her vigil. If and when he woke, she told herself, she had to be there.

The pool room's atmosphere started to seep into her. The quiet cool airiness. It began to seem more spacious than the whole of the rest of the island, and somehow more real as well. When she wasn't feeding, cleaning or turning him, she would pace tirelessly around him. Hour after hour. It felt like year after year.

At these dreamiest of times she saw his couch as a funeral plinth. Once she even fancied that there wasn't one of them but two. She saw herself weaving between them, trying to measure out both, to compare their shapes and sizes. This other plinth could only have been Arthur's. Even if he weren't truly dead, she needed to picture him laid out, primed for the grave.

Arthur. Still he haunted her. The black cross rising. Those two muscled birth-welts high on his back, marking him out in biblical style as the king he would one day be. And she saw him seeping ashore to hunt her down and begin it all again. But he never really had to hunt her, even in her waking dreams. Even there she had no escape.

In that seamless sequence of days and nights, the king and the sleeper merged in Morgan's mind – convincing her finally that the latter was a merlin, an Arthur's Man. Every merlin, after all, seemed to have only Arthur's air running through him, emerging in words to shape the chaos. But this one stayed silent. And Morgan liked that, she wanted it to go on – at least until she had unburdened herself of all her past pain. This, she was starting to believe, was the point of their being together.

After a week she left the villa for the first time.

It was dawn, and she had spent the night before on a couch near the merlin. The soft, hoarse roar of the ocean had threaded all her sleep, its one-word song seeming to rise from the pool as well as the shore. A word of two syllables, cresting on the first and then falling away. Not 'confess' but something odder. *Log-res . . . Log-res . . .* It had sounded like a summons.

She walked out thoughtfully to the cliff top. The morning was warm, the dew already dry underfoot. She heard a faint drone of flies below but kept her gaze high for a while. After staring at the water till her eyes began to sting, she looked down.

In the light of what Anna had said, she had already guessed what she would see, but the sight still astonished her.

The fact that it was happening in this pearly morning glow made it more disarming still. It seemed to have been plucked from under the cover of night, where by right it belonged. By day it looked brazenly shameless.

Directly under the cliff-face, where the scrub was pocked with cairns, the women sat scattered among half a dozen male corpses. Three of the bodies were smeary-dark with mud. They must have been disinterred. None of the merlins dumped by the sea had ever looked so sordid . . . *Sometimes they dig them up . . .* For a moment Morgan was inexplicably grateful that her own man hadn't had to be buried. *Play with them . . .*

'Play' wasn't the word Morgan would have chosen. The women looked so businesslike. Maybe this was just Morgan's own squeamishness, but she couldn't believe they were doing it of their own free will. It seemed impossible that, without orders, anyone could have behaved in that way.

Only one of the women was using a body for a familiar

38

form of pleasure. With her watery-red dress bunched at her waist, she sat straight-backed across its abdomen. She was riding it so hard that twice she toppled forward.

She regained her balance by grabbing splay-fingered first at the shoulder, then at the head. Morgan watched in wonder as she pushed her finger into an eye-socket just to recover herself. When she'd finished she slumped and rolled aside, wearily swatting the curved, death-stiffened penis out of her.

Around her the others, undistracted, were slicing and stitching. Not much blood seemed to have spilled from where they had cut out each man's sexual parts. Morgan wondered what kind of a thread they were using to sew the hardened slabs of flesh into the lips and cheeks. The bone needles they were stabbing with looked small, but obviously they were sturdy.

Morgan watched as if from a different Age, startled by her own calmness. *The end of Albion* . . . she thought, newly intrigued. And the merlins must all have died excited. She felt no nausea, no outrage. There was such a busy kind of innocence about the women. And the longer she looked, the more it seemed to be expressing about what she herself had left behind, what she no longer needed to fear. Their thread was like a line across her life, separating the bad from the good.

And the seven themselves were good. Morgan saw them as a kind of school class, learning a new accomplishment on a collection of life-sized human dolls. There really seemed to be more romance here than ritual. And to add to this impression, Anna then wandered into view from further up the shore.

The girl carried a dark plume of seaweed that she swished at the cairns as she passed. She didn't try to skirt round the women, who in turn ignored her. She looked like a tiny supervisor picking her way between them, pausing sometimes to peer closer and, once or twice, to flick at a corpse's head with her seaweed.

Again Morgan was struck by her poise, her silent, faintly contemptuous self-possession. When she had gone beyond them all, she stopped, turned, and looked straight up at Morgan.

She smiled so broadly; all her little features seemed to bunch at the limits of her grin. Morgan barely managed to stop herself smiling back. She looked instead at the corpses, but she saw only her own survivor back in the villa. His crucified posture down there on the first day. *You will have everything you need* . . .

Her hand moved of its own accord to the band on her upper arm, which for once was uncovered by her wrap. She turned to go back to the villa, then heard a scampering on the cliff-path behind her.

'You came to see them playing,' Anna panted, falling into step. She had dropped the swatch of seaweed and swung her arms as she walked. She sounded pleased, as if she had proved a point.

Morgan said nothing. Words were beyond her. At least about what they were now leaving behind. She smiled down at Anna. You're two in one, she thought. Woman and child. Like a tree on fire down one side only.

'What's that?' the girl said, bringing Morgan back to herself.

Anna was pointing at her golden armlet. Morgan glanced at it, as if she herself had only just noticed it was there. She walked on in silence for a few steps, wondering what to say; it seemed like the right time to say something. Finally she grasped the thing, twisted it once, then slid it past her elbow and over her wrist. Immediately she felt lighter.

'There,' she said, passing it down. 'It's just a bangle. A piece of jewellery. But take care with the eye . . .'

Anna took it dubiously, then fed it round and round in her hands. 'It looks like that bird that pecked the statue,' she suggested, 'only not the same colour.'

'It's a dragon,' Morgan told her. She paused, knelt down and pointed at the wide-jawed face, wishing that she'd had more practice at talking to children. 'Look, it's swallowing its own tail. Can you see the wings folded tight to its body? And the claws underneath? So many parts to it, all squashed together to make a ring of gold. Do you like it?'

It was easy to speak. *Just a bangle.* She had almost managed to convince herself. But Anna wouldn't answer her question.

She prodded the single eye's blood-red hardness. 'What is it made of?'

'Something called garnet. But do you like it?' Morgan asked her a second time.

Anna used her tongue to hook a hang of hair into her mouth. 'It's frightening.'

Morgan, kneeling back, nodded her head. This waif strolled the shore watching dead men's members being grafted on to their faces, and yet she found this trinket frightening. But Morgan knew that she was right to be afraid.

'The king gave it to me,' she said, as if this in itself explained the ominousness.

'The king?'

'You know, in . . . Albion? King Arthur?'

It hadn't been so much a gift as an acknowledgement. All through the wars against the Sea Wolves, Arthur's need had lain curled up before her like a beast just pretending to be asleep. That was surely why he had given her the band: a golden dragon swallowing itself, seemingly at rest but with one eye open. He gave it to her at the wars' end. The wars which he had risen from obscurity to win almost single-handed. He gave it without a word. A priest watching close by had asked to see it before Morgan slipped it on. He had held it in trembling fingers as if it might rear up and swallow him too. 'The beast,' he had murmured. 'The beast that was, and is not, and yet is.'

'Arthur,' Anna repeated, staring hard at the dragon. 'But he is not a real king.' She seemed to want to keep even the idea of him at bay.

'Oh, he's real,' Morgan assured her, wondering whether the girl believed in half of the things she said, or if she said them merely to provoke.

'But I have heard about him in the tales. He had the mark to show that he was a true-born ruler. And he won all the wars. But then in the peace he stopped being a proper king. So his son came back and killed him.'

Morgan let herself laugh. Tales, stories. Wherever there were merlins, there were legends about Arthur – even when the merlins themselves were dead. Maybe the air that contained all the tales no longer needed to pass through them first in order to be heard.

'No. You're confusing him,' Morgan said. 'Arthur had no son . . . Not one old enough to kill him . . .'

She could say that too. She closed her eyes and saw the black cross but it wasn't so close; a speck in the distance now. *Everything you need* . . . She was safe here. To her, he really might just as well have been dead.

She smiled at Anna, who was still spellbound by the armlet. 'Try it on. Go ahead.'

Anna eyed its width, looked at her own bony little arm and shrugged. Then with a giggle she raised one leg, passed it over her foot and tried to lodge it high on her thigh. Still it was far too big.

Morgan watched, delighted. This was just what she needed. To share the grisly thing. Demystify it.

No one else had ever touched it. No one since him. Lose the baby, keep the bauble, she had thought as the boat left the kingdom. She had given up his second gift to her, but hadn't dared to give up the first. By keeping it, she had hoped in some irrational way to keep its giver at bay. She still did. But Anna's little joke now at least made it easier to wear. She took it back and eased it over her wrist again.

Anna had bent over. She spat on her finger and rubbed

hard at her thigh where the dragon had been. 'What is it?' asked Morgan. 'What's the matter?'

The girl straightened up with a muted grin. 'That dragon, it messed on my leg.'

Morgan smiled, twisting the armlet upward, chafing her soft shoulder-skin as it bit home. She had hardly heard the girl's joke. She was remembering the woman on the shore rocking herself back and forth. It had seemed to make so much sense at the time, seemed in its way almost beautiful. More beautiful than anything she had known herself with men . . .

Slowly they walked together up the gentle gradient past the villa. They were leaving the sea behind, yet Morgan felt as if she were walking on water. She often did. It was partly to do with the quality of the light. The rising sun's rays seemed to be reflected back by the leaves. The more distant fields shimmered in the hazy breeze like a lake's ruffled surface. At times like this, Morgan felt sure that she was still on her outward voyage.

Just before the gate of the nearest apple orchard, she cried out as a bolt of pain stabbed her stomach.

'What is it? What is it?' Anna was prancing anxiously at her side.

Morgan shook her head. Gathering herself, she turned and gazed back down at the villa. It seemed to be floating in the day's first heat. There was no reason not to answer. Not now.

'I had a child,' she said to the slope. 'Not long ago . . .'

'A baby?' Anna asked, seeming to bridle.

44

'A son.'

'What was he called?'

Morgan smiled. 'There wasn't time to give him a name.'

'How old is he now? Not older than me?'

'No, not older than you. He's probably not even alive. He was taken, you see, as soon as he was born. Just before I was sent here.'

Her eyes stung but her voice was even. A son, but not her own. Guenever had been so keen to stress that fact in trying to console her. A son of nothing – of less than nothing. Rainspits were gusting in the sunshine as Morgan started to make her way back to the villa.

'Who took him?' Anna asked.

'The king's wife.' She looked away. 'To try to keep him safe.'

'From what?'

From what. Not from whom. Which was just about right. From what the merlins had said he would become. *A seed sown in darkness will surely blossom in an evil way* . . . Morgan shrugged, her throat suddenly swollen. She touched her armlet, as if that might act as an answer.

'From what? Don't you know?' Anna was walking a little way behind now. Morgan heard her scuffing up dust with her heels. The rain was coming harder.

She shook her head. 'Yes, I do know. But it wouldn't make sense to you.' It made little enough sense to Morgan herself, even now. It was like speaking about someone else entirely, some other bereaved mother in a far distant land.

Anna paused before speaking again. 'He probably is alive,' she then said briskly. 'If I had somebody's baby to look after, I would keep him alive.' She sounded as if she were taking Morgan to task for doubting it.

'Yes,' Morgan answered, reaching behind her, flexing her fingers, and finally feeling the girl's hand slip into her own. 'I'm sure you would.'

She let the tears roll down her face as they walked on in silence through the strange squally rain that seemed to swirl up from the ground, not fall from the sky. At the villa's outer wall Anna pulled away and skipped back towards the cliff top without saying another word.

With folded arms, Morgan passed through to the courtyard. It had helped to speak. She guessed that now she would have no more sudden pangs in her abdomen.

She tilted back her head to feel the rain on her face. The stained statue stared back down. It seemed like aeons since the cormorant had been up there. The past was falling away more abruptly than ever. It was as if everything that happened came rolling down the slope from the hinterland, slipped over the cliff and was swallowed by the deep.

She stayed out of doors, fitfully crying, until all the clouds had gone. Then she went inside to prepare her merlin's meal.

Throughout the morning, the sights she had seen on the dawn shore had been growing more vivid in her mind. But the face on every corpse had been his; their limbs had all been his as well.

She pulled off most of her sodden clothes before going in to him.

Again for a moment she thought she saw cuts on his exposed flesh. Bigger than before, with blood dripping down. *Not my blood . . .* It was another mirage but her eyes never really deceived her, and it made her tremble constantly as she cleaned then fed him. And all the while his features kept blurring with Arthur's underneath her. Which wasn't so surprising. If she cared to look close enough, there were plenty of ways in which he resembled the king as a younger man. His noble nose, the jut of his jaw, the delicacy of his wrists under such lengthy forearms, but most of all the mass and feel of his hair. All that hair . . .

By the time she had finished, she felt as if the king's gritty shadow had seeped back to swallow her whole. Suddenly exhausted, she crawled across to her own couch and curled up on it. But she couldn't sleep; couldn't get away like that. Nor could she keep the memories back. And in the end, for the first time during her exile, she gave up trying to stem them.

His wild, blind madness gripped her again. Waging his old dead war by other means. Fanning the conflict back into flames. Shooting his fire up into her as once he had scorched great grids of earth in his wars. A hundred men on just one horse; a thousand with a single weapon . . .

Morgan choked on her tears. Retched, gagged, whimpered. But on it rushed inside her, unstoppered, up from the darkness and into her light:

He would pin her down, then rear up high. Blood

47

and hair and murder above her, holding her steady with great savage hands. She had barely dared to breathe. His eyes would be closed, but then eyeless he searched her. Peering past her heart for his target.

Then he would find it, and drive himself in. Higher and higher, as if to burn her clean. Calculated erasure. Obliteration with intent. And always before he came, he would tear himself away. Time after time. Turn from her and spill his seed. And then she would see that great dark cross convulsing on his back . . .

But whatever he tried to kill would each time grow again – to be tracked and sighted and burned out anew. Night after night after night. Until at last she had held him fast. Just once. *He'll stop if you're pregnant*, Guenever had told her. The beast in him was squeamish too. And so, in that way, Morgan had put herself beyond his need, and shattered the ghastly cycle.

It's not your son . . . In one sense, of course, Guenever was right. The child when it came had been a sign, not a son, a principle, not a person. The merlins had seen to that. It belonged to them all: all – including Guenever – who had endured the true brutishness of Arthur's 'Age of Gold' and dreamed of a reprieve. But it had been a baby too. It *had* been Morgan's. And she had let it go . . . long, long before its birth.

She wept hard on her couch now, gripping the armlet as if to hide her own darker side from the dragon's garnet eye. As the shudders subsided she looked across at the sleeper. A merlin, but a man as well. More of a man than those creatures on the beach. For her, she knew, it could have been worse. He could have been hurt. He could have been awake and insane with pain. He could have been hideous.

Morgan stood and crossed to his couch. She ran the back of her hand from his temple to his neck. The feel of him peeved her. A slab of cool meat on a plinth. Yet once she had approached as if this were an altar, afraid that he might be a dream.

A seed sown in darkness . . . The merlins, the merlins. Morgan the false, they had called her. Morgan the fateful, Morgan the Fay . . . They had said she worked on Arthur with her demon's eyes. Made him 'not himself'. Turned him into that beast for her own filthy reasons. And all on one climactic night! As if he hadn't already forced her a hundred times before.

A seed, a seed, a seed . . . That was the most sordid distortion of all. Their son could have been seen as Arthur's heir, not marked out as his nemesis. Before the child had ever left her, the merlins had ensured that it wouldn't stay alive.

She took a fistful of the trickster's hair and rubbed it in his unresisting face. She imagined herself stuffing it into his mouth and nose until all the life was stifled out of him. Arthur's Man. She wanted him gone – much as, in her heart, she had wanted her baby to be ripped away. She admitted that now. She could own up to everything here, she could do whatever she chose. This was her castle, she was its queen, this sleeping hero was her hostage.

She leaned over and dripped a string of saliva into his eye-socket.

49

In her dream he had wailed that he was a murderer. Only in her dream. He was no killer. He was no Arthur. Killing was not his condition, as always it was with the king. This man's hands were made for wringing together, not for wringing necks. She despised him. She spat on him again and left the room. That night, she slept in her own quarters.

Then the next day came.

FOUR

Morgan waited till nightfall before feeding him. All day long she had known what would happen. In her heart of hearts she had known since the day he had arrived. They were both here for a reason. This had to be it.

Instead of using the lanterns or candles, she dragged the brazier closer to the couch to see him better by its glow. She tipped the liquid into him with a steady hand. Her nerve stayed firm; she wouldn't back out now.

She stood, set aside the dishes, and circled him slowly in her usual way. His tunic was clean, which pleased her. Not all of her spit had dried on his eye. His right hand lay palm upward at his side, exactly where she had last released it.

She knelt next to it and grasped his wrist with one of her own hands. Then, supporting his knuckles with the other, she began to run her tongue across his wintry fingers.

After so long, her appetite was huge. But like a favourite meal, this had to be properly prepared. She wanted him wetter. Dry, he was still too distant, and his faint smell of fires was too earthbound. She longed for him to be soused in salt shore-water. She closed her eyes and saw him as he had been in her dream: walking through the waves, sea-slick, reaching up but never quite touching.

She nudged his fingers apart and took one after another into her mouth, sucking them down to the knuckle, gently kneading his smoky skin with her teeth.

He didn't respond and she didn't expect him to. Not yet. But he felt more alive under her tongue than in her hands. She sensed the speed inside him now; his distant rush to the surface of himself. It had to be like this. Soon, she knew, he would be with her, to take what remained of her pain.

She raised herself a little. Leaning against the couch, she went on working at his fingers while reaching up to feel his face. His lips were already apart and she eased her fingers inside. His tongue seemed to shift, making a wider passage, as if he expected her to reach down and wrench out his sleeping soul. But Morgan just wanted his saliva, which she smeared on his lips, his bearded cheekbones, his eyes.

Her own eyes stayed on his hand. Still it intrigued her. In her dream he had seemed to be brandishing it at her. Maybe it had held a knife. The hand he had said he had killed with. But the blood had been on her. His blood, hers, the king's: theirs.

Now she understood what that had meant. He had been offering himself. Asking to take back what he and his kind had given her. The hurt and the blood and distortions. The truth of it rose like steam from the body she was moistening.

She took her hand from the merlin's face, licked it herself and dampened his other hand. Then, wetting herself again, she reached down to the hem of his unsoiled tunic.

His knees were inches apart. Morgan slid her palm between and stroked one inner thigh, then the other. His skin was even cooler there. He might have flinched as her hand went high each time, but by now her own heart was beating too hard for her to be sure. She remembered how in her childbed Guenever had coaxed her legs further apart, murmuring above her own screams: 'Soon now, soon . . .'

She stopped short of his groin, intending to wet him there in a different way. Working again at his legs, she raised herself higher, virtually lying beside him now on the couch, bringing her mouth close to his ear. Close enough to whisper, if not to kiss.

There was so much she wanted to say. A lifetime's worth of words. Purging herself, first of the merlins' own slanders; sending them back and burying them. Then telling the mazier truth about what she really was and what she'd never been. She needed him to hear her truth.

But no words came. Just the shapes that made them. He was still too far away, too deep inside himself. She had to bring him higher. The words would follow the wetness. First she had to soak him.

Morgan swung herself on to the couch. It was wide enough for the two of them, as she had known it would be. Plinth, dais: it had been waiting for them both. She closed her hand around his nearer thigh as her head settled softly on the cushion next to his. Already their hair was tangling. She closed her eyes and was back in her childbed. The baby was being dragged away. *It's not your son . . . I'll keep him safe . . . You'll have everything you need . . .*

'No more Arthur,' Morgan murmured at the merlin, starting to cut the cord that tied her to that old bad world.

Inside her tiny echo, the dragon-armlet pinned beneath her seemed to grip her more tightly. And then she felt the release, deep in her chest.

'Not Arthur. No more Arthur. Never more Arthur. Arthur, Arthur, Arthur . . .'

Breathless, she went on. Repeating his name till in the end what she was hearing was 'Rather'. Which made her smile, then stop. The king was so hard to see inside all the legends, so many things to so many different people. Even his name could mutate into a word suggesting some alternative.

'The king is dead,' she said to herself through the merlin. It was as if he had spoken the words to her. And now she believed him. This, for her, was the end of Albion.

She drew away just far enough to hitch up her gown,

and untie the sash that held her aching breasts. Already both were soaked. The fluid dribbled in rivulets, grey on to the sleeper's arm, dark against the couch's fabric.

Morgan swung herself across him and straddled his stomach. Then she leaned forward to push herself into his face, expressing her milk into his eyes and hair. Finally she cupped his head towards her, fed one nipple between his lips and let his teeth hold her gently.

She felt nothing. Nothing that didn't come from herself. She rolled her teat inside his mouth to make more milk come. It felt right, as if she had done it over and over again. She felt no sadness for the lost child she should have fed; it hadn't been her son. She had all she wanted. She didn't even need her milk to be flowing into this sleeping surrogate, just as long as it came; and this seemed the quickest, surest way to empty herself.

When his mouth began to overflow, she drew back and let her gown fall over her. She eased back further and felt the tip of his erection against her bottom.

She felt no surprise nor shock. She had known he would respond to her in the end. Ever since she had first touched his hand with Anna watching. Just by looking she could enthrall any man — the best and the worst of them — if only she let herself do it.

He was solid through the coarse wool of his tunic and the silk of her own gown. Morgan knelt up to lift its skirt to her waist; under it she was naked. She lowered herself on to him again, keeping most of her weight on her knees. This time she sat lightly across his still-covered penis, then she began to move back and forth.

She drew no purely sexual charge from him, but there was a powerfully soothing pleasure in feeling him against her. A restorative thrill, as if she were drinking a potion to make some lifelong disease in her blood disappear. She closed her eyes, not wanting to acknowledge that he was there, that he had his own role in any of this.

As the strain on her legs began to tell, she let him take more of her weight. His hardness was a balm, fully healing at least the physical hurts of her childbirth. But each stroke went further too. It brought back her body bone by bone from its strange post-natal limbo. She felt as if she were coming together in a new way on top of him. As someone who would be better equipped than the old Morgan to live with whatever came after.

She had made his tunic wetter than she liked now. With her eyes closed, she reached between her legs and plucked it up out of her way. Her hand brushed his scrotum, bulbous and hot. Higher, she let her fingers linger. He was as ready as she was, filmy for her, but still elsewhere he was glacial.

Morgan bent forward to kiss his mouth. His lips and teeth moved apart for her tongue. The taste of her own milk was good, familiar, and distinctive enough to be untainted by his smokiness.

Each twist and turn of her blind reconnaisance pleased her. Each frisson drew her in deeper. She realized only then that she had been looking for reasons to stop, to be distracted, repelled, to convince herself that what she really wanted couldn't be so blatant. But here, now, for the newly re-made Morgan, nothing but this was possible.

She kissed his eyes, then she reached back again and lifted him and slid him up into her. When he was as high as she needed, she straightened and looked down. She had thought she might soak him in tears, but her need to cry had passed. First her need to speak, then her need to weep. She kept very still, holding him so loosely that she felt his blood pulse inside her. His blood, hers . . .

His face was too far down to touch. She had to keep this balance. But she wanted to touch him, *for* him – fondly and furiously, like a mother suddenly confronted by a small son who had been out of her sight for too long, a son about whom she had begun to fear the worst. She remembered his guilty hand coming up in her dream. He needed her warmth, her forgiveness.

But the new Morgan would put no man's needs before her own. With splayed fingers she steadied herself against his shoulders, then gripped him below as if she planned to throttle him. She brought herself to his hilt, then sank back down, so slowly that every last grain of time on this island seemed to have been tipped away into the sea.

In those two protracted movements she travelled to Arthur's Albion and all the way back again. Travelled by sea. The sea that had swallowed this sleeper and then spat him out. The sea that Morgan still sensed simmering inside this island of her exile, and inside the sleeper too instead of blood. The sea that would break from him soon, soon now . . .

She floated on top of him, softly dashed by the waves of him. Open-mouthed, she grinned as the man beneath her tensed bodily. Then she twisted her hips quickly to drag out his short warm orgasm.

He made no sound. Nor did she. Already in her mind she had moved away from him, away from all of this. She had what she wanted. His heartless kind had violated her; now she had done the same to him. It needed to happen only once.

She closed her eyes as he subsided. Albion had ended. It hadn't been like sex at all, hadn't affected her like sex. She had relished it precisely because it hadn't engaged her emotions. She felt no shame, only new strength. A first gentle flexing of the powers that the merlins had accused her of misusing. Maybe, after all, she could be a Fay, channelling the charge in herself towards new, undreamed-of ends.

But smiling through her tiredness, she was thrilled to be a woman – and this particular woman too. The only woman she could be. Totally self-sufficient, seizing her second chance, moving over men like stones in a causeway till at last she arrived where she was awaited.

Before going forward, she took a last glimpse back. *It's not your son . . .* She saw Guenever's earnest eyes. Nothing now stood between Morgan and the memory. She saw Arthur's wife holding the newborn May baby; the child that could never have escaped Arthur and his levy men. But her grieving days were over. She felt too alive. As wild as lightning. It had all been a part of Albion, and Albion now had been ended, here, for ever. She didn't even look back at the merlin as she slid down to leave the room.

Morgan went to the fountain, undressed, and splashed herself with water. Face, arms and breasts, but not between her legs. Not yet. Those traces were her own. For as long as it had taken, the penis had been hers as much as his. She had sided with it against its supine owner; driven it deeper and deeper until she had come for them both.

Now she was clean. Free. A queen.

Morgan slept soundly that night and for most of the next day. But she rose feeling sluggish and a little uncertain. The sea seemed to beat louder under the cliff; the villa's atmosphere was too deeply still.

At sunset she went out to pick vegetables for the merlin's gruel; but once in the kitchens, she couldn't chop them up. So much time seemed to have passed since the evening before. She couldn't believe that the merlin would still be there. Or, if he was, that he could still be alive.

Tremulous, still gripping the vegetable knife, she crossed to the pool room. She felt as if she were wading through water to get there. As she entered, she saw his stretched-out silhouette.

She drifted closer, expecting to find him yellowed with death, his erection intact like one of the shore corpse's. But he had just slept on, flaccid, filthy. Below his rucked-up tunic, thin cormorant-like stains lined his thighs. Morgan closed in, ignoring the smell.

On his face and mane her milk had dried into pale flakes. Gazing down, she knew that she couldn't look after him any more. She had outgrown him now, left him behind, drawn his sting. Never again would a merlin have anything to say to her, or about her, or against her.

She pressed the flat of the knife to her leg. Then on an impulse she grabbed a heap of his hair and chopped it off.

Another great handful followed. Another. It came off so easily. Again she felt the power course through her. Six strokes later, he had nothing but coal-black tufts all over his head. Morgan blew the mess from his face and tossed the knife into the water. It was over. She felt that she had changed not just his appearance, but a whole lot more inside herself.

She turned away from the pool, and belatedly realized that two of the lanterns had been lit. Then she saw Anna fast asleep on the smaller beige pool-side couch that she had sometimes used herself. The girl's small, fleshy mouth was wide open and slightly twisted against the couch's raised end, which was darkened by her dribble.

Morgan felt too tired to be startled. *Play* . . . she thought. Maybe Anna had been there the night before as well, watching from one of the corners. Maybe all the women had been watching, like official observers of her own fresh start. Making sure she did at last what she was meant to do.

She made her way across, and gently lowered herself on to the couch beside the girl. For several minutes she sat stroking her angry fizz of hair. Anna's hairline was high, and the veins at her left temple were vividly blue. She looked so vulnerable now. Such a little scrap.

Soon Morgan's eyes began to close, her head to rock. She swung up her legs and stretched out on her back next to the tiny curled form.

They stayed in parallel, barely touching, for hours. Neither moved; the girl slept on, Morgan dozed. Through it all she asked herself what she should be feeling, what this should be meaning to her. For so long her instinct had been to push others away, to resist any deep kind of intimacy.

She wished, if anything, that Anna were older; already a woman, with her own female wariness of whatever world they now had to share. She might have embraced her then – put out an arm and enfolded her, just while she slept. But she didn't hold Anna, just as she had never really held Guenever, her sister in suffering. It still wasn't in her to hold another living soul.

Finally she eased herself off the couch and tiptoed away. The lanterns had guttered. In the gloom she turned and looked back from the colonnade. Anna was still in the same position, but her eyes were wide and unblearily open. She stared so hard through the murk that Morgan let out a small laugh.

'Did you just wake?' she asked. 'Or were you never asleep?' Immediately she began to wonder how real the merlin's sleep was too.

Anna didn't answer. Instead she raised herself on to one elbow and pointed at Morgan's armlet, which had been left exposed by her nightdress.

'It was true what I told you before,' the girl called. 'The king did try to put his baby in the sea, but the baby was saved. And the king went in a hole in his own hill to hide. But when the baby grew into a man, he came and killed the king. It's *true* . . .' Her voice cracked, as if the sick little story really mattered.

Morgan stared back. This was meant to be a new beginning, her second chance. Suddenly the girl's face looked so old. Morgan covered the armlet with her hand and said softly, 'Kings don't harm babies. Why should a king want to harm a little baby?'

Anna blinked. Morgan heard the echo of her answer even before she quoted the all-too-familiar words: '"A seed sown in darkness will surely blossom in an evil way."'

Morgan blanched, then glanced over at the merlin. 'Do you know what that means?'

Anna just rested her head again, curled up tighter, and stuffed her mouth with hair – quite possibly to show that she didn't want it to be severed like the merlin's. Morgan went back to her quarters, abandoning them both. In that bad moment she resented the child almost as much as she resented the man.

She slept right through to the following sunset, when the song of the sea aroused her again. Its call sounded more urgent than ever. *Logres . . . Logres . . . Logres . . .* Throwing on her wrap, she heaved herself barefoot out to the villa's forecourt. If she had been floating before, she now felt quite definitely that she was moving lower in the water.

All seven women were heading towards her from the cliff-top.

62

FIVE

Morgan pulled her wrap tight and made herself taller to face the women. The sun's last rays made them look almost transparent as they approached. Behind them the sound of the sea came on, like an eighth person.

'We could have him now,' called the leading woman from some distance. She spoke Morgan's language so competently that she sounded almost irritated.

She was ten steps ahead of the rest. Sallower even than them, stooped, skinny, maybe three times their age, with low slingshot breasts loose inside her dress. But still she had a stealthy beauty. 'If you no longer want him with you, we could take him back.'

Morgan smiled. How did they know? From Anna? And what would they take him back to? The softly baying sea? Or would they simply bury him alive? Morgan's mind was racing. I have power now, she tried to tell herself, yet the women's mere presence seemed to have diluted it already.

'So you can speak,' she noted coolly.

The leader stopped two men's lengths away. She nodded her head, and did not seem inclined to elaborate. Her stance – splay-footed, head held low on her shoulders – reminded Morgan of one of the younger women she had faced down on the shore. Her calf-length dress was also the same washed-out shade of yellow. It looked as if it had gone to ruin on her over a period of decades.

'We could take him,' she said. 'If that's what you would prefer now.'

Now, now. Morgan twisted the armlet under her wrap. Now that she had exorcized herself on him? Why else was now any different from before? She pointed one foot in front of her and tried to describe an arc in the dust between them. She felt crowded, clumsy, breathless. And although she was still bobbing buoyant here before them, she seemed also to be skeetering forward in time, leaving all this behind before it had even happened.

'So: shall we take him?'

'Yes,' Morgan told the ground. 'Yes, I think that might be best . . . now.'

The six looked to their leader, who nodded. At once they fanned out and made for the villa. Morgan watched them ripple past, the water women: some were familiar, some not. She wondered vaguely if they were all related.

The seventh stayed put, her chin touching her breast-bone, apparently deep in thought; she looked a little like a resting heron. Morgan felt time moving ever faster around herself. The land at her back had surely steepened. The moments tore past into the insatiable sea. *Logres* . . . echoed at her as each wave rose and fell, *Logres, Logres* . . .

'Why did he have to come here in the first place?' she asked the woman with a smile, not so much out of curiosity as to confirm what she had worked out for herself.

'To this island or to the villa?'

'Both.'

'For you to be with him.'

Be with. The woman tilted her head to emphasize the euphemism. She clearly wasn't talking about feeding and cleaning. I have power, Morgan reminded herself, and it echoed in her head like a joke.

'For me to be with? Was that why he came here? Or did you just decide when he arrived?'

'We decide nothing. You've been made to do nothing here.' She paused, and for a moment looked rueful. 'You have done what you thought was right.'

'Who are you?' Morgan asked as levelly as she could. 'What are you? Why are you here in this place? Just what is it that you do?'

'My name is Moronoe. The others and I mark the boundaries. We show where it begins.'

'What? Where what begins?'

'Everything. All that is not in the water.'

Morgan blinked, infuriated. These sounded like lines from some arcane catechism, and they were no use to her at all. 'What is this place?' she snarled. 'Where in the name of God am I?'

The heron-woman uncoiled her neck. 'If you mean what do people call the island, for the most part I'd say Avalon. Some prefer the Summer Country.' She shrugged and frowned, as if she had been sworn to make her replies as full as possible. 'Then again, there are those who call it the Land of Women.'

Morgan arched an eyebrow. She had heard of the Land of Women; the merlins had located some of their more fanciful post-war stories there. She had always thought it was a kind of faery underworld, the land of the fortunate dead.

'*Are* there only women here?'

The woman gestured at the villa, where the others were presumably now scrubbing down someone who was patently male. Morgan drew another arc in the dust with her foot. Her head reeled. She sensed that this woman would tell her everything if pressed. This wasn't like questioning Anna. But she wasn't yet sure if she was ready to hear all the answers.

She made a short, straight line in the dust. 'So what kind of an island is this?' she asked. 'A penal colony?'

'Does it seem like that to you?'

'No,' Morgan said, 'no, it doesn't.' She noticed that the woman hadn't asked her why she might have felt any punishment was due. 'But what happens here? What goes on?'

'Avalon is the place where all things begin and end,' the woman said softly before looking away. 'It's where everything finally turns into itself.'

Another bit of catechism. Morgan needed straighter answers. 'Is it a part of Arthur's kingdom?'

She flushed on the king's name and saw that the woman had noticed. She'd seen, too, that Morgan's three strokes on the ground had formed the letter 'A'. She tilted her head again, as if by looking at Morgan from a different angle she could make what she said next sound more convincing:

'You have already been told about Arthur.'

Morgan snorted. 'You mean that he's dead? Killed by his own son!'

The woman glanced away. She seemed disinclined to argue. Morgan knew that there was no going back now. 'Why am I here?' she asked dizzily. 'Tell me, truly. Was it you who brought me here? Why? Say!'

The woman ducked her head, as if she were letting the questions arrow out over her shoulder, past the cliff-top and into the waiting water. But then she answered quite calmly: 'You were brought here so that, in time, you could be with him,' and she tipped her head towards the villa.

'Be with! Be with! But *why?* Why here? Why not in, oh, Albion?'

'Albion has ended. Nothing you have been told here is untrue.'

'Ended? A kingdom? And all the people in it? All Arthur's people?'

The woman nodded. 'They are waiting now. Except for the merlins, as you have seen.'

'Waiting for what?'

'To come through. At the Great Remaking. When the new kingdom comes.'

Morgan smiled as the world teemed around her. Under the blackened sky, the sea sounded so much closer. She wanted to believe that this woman really knew nothing; that she and the others were just half-witted outcasts, patrolling the shore for no one but themselves, playing mating games for others when their own perversions palled. But it wouldn't ring true.

Feigning indifference, she asked, 'You know, of course, who I am?'

Who, not what. But she did need to know now. She could live with whatever she heard, even if it was 'Morgan the Fay'. And if she was known to them as the king's mistress, and the mother of his bastard son, then so be it. She knew the truth herself. So now did the sleeper. Besides, what king in history *hadn't* sired sons outside his marriage?

The woman paused before answering. 'Yes, we know.' Then a small cloud passed over her features. 'At least, we know who you *were*.'

Please, thought Morgan. No more word-play. 'What do you mean?'

The woman eyed her as if in pity, but with distaste as well, and maybe even incredulity.

'Say!' Morgan cried, racked by her silence. 'What do you mean?'

'That you were once the sister of Arthur.'

She sounded hesitant, but only out of politeness.

For a beat Morgan thought that the woman had used the word which she had been expecting: 'Mistress.' But she hadn't said 'mistress'. The word 'sister' stunned her. It was so long since Morgan had seen herself in that way. Years. A lifetime.

Morgan smiled, curling her toes under her gown's hem. '"Once,"' she repeated. 'And I no longer am? Because you say that he's dead?'

The woman tilted her head. 'Because I say that you no longer are. Not his . . . sister.'

She accentuated the last word with a sympathetic shrug, but her eyes were meeting Morgan's too levelly. *We know who you were* . . . Guenever had confronted her in just the same way. 'I know what you are to him,' she had said. 'I'm his sister,' Morgan had gasped. 'His sister,' Guenever had agreed. 'His . . . *sister*.' And in those two neutral words she had somehow encompassed the entire enormity of it.

Morgan made to touch her stomach, but couldn't go through with the movement. The woman stayed stock still. She seemed quite ready to find Morgan sceptical, abusive, even violent.

'How would you know about any of this?' Morgan laughed. 'Who tells you? The merlins?'

The woman who had called herself Moronoe stared back sadly. Morgan recalled how the seven had been desecrating the merlins' corpses down by the sea. And the merlins in the kingdom had never shown the slightest interest in any woman; it hardly seemed likely now that these two singular sets of people should be in league.

She narrowed her eyes, remembering how she had ridden her own captive by the poolside. 'Why do you want him back?' she asked. 'The merlin in the villa?'

'He's not a merlin.'

'What?' Morgan didn't know whether to feel affronted or afraid.

'He is not the same as the others.'

Morgan looked back to the villa. He wasn't a merlin. She wondered, inanely, if she had stopped him from being one just by cutting off his hair. There was still no sign of the women bringing him out; she couldn't think what was keeping them. She closed her eyes tight. 'Who is he then?'

'He is Mordred.'

Morgan looked at her and she nodded back, as if willing her to believe it. But the name was no more familiar to Morgan than 'Avalon' had been. 'He ended your brother's kingdom.'

Morgan frowned. Such awkward language . . . and so evasive. There seemed to be only one way to end a kingdom. 'You're trying to tell me he killed Arthur?' she sneered. 'Like you told the little girl that his own "son" killed him?'

'He ended your brother's kingdom,' the woman solemnly repeated. 'The king was made for that kingdom, and Mordred ended it. Now we have a second chance. The next kingdom will be different. It will be made for the king.'

Morgan shook her head, unable and unwilling to follow. The phrase 'a second chance' rang inside her head. She felt so unsure, cheated, horribly betrayed by more than just her own instincts. She tried to smile, to go back to the lesser, more immediate issue.

'The man in there. Mordred, you call him. You say that he's here because of me?'

'He belonged with you, yes.'

'And he doesn't now?' She glared at the sky.

'Not unless you want him.'

'Why not? What makes things any different now?'

'Your condition.'

Morgan narrowed her eyes. 'What?'

'The child inside you.'

'You think I'm pregnant!'

The woman didn't nod her head so much as tilt it further, as if to take a corrective slap to the cheek. Morgan laughed; a harsh little rasp.

Then she heard movement at the villa's entrance, and she turned and peered through the dark. First two of the women came out, empty-handed, followed at widening intervals by the other four. The dreamy way that they walked showed their helplessness even before they came within speaking range.

He's dead, thought Morgan with a sad surprising thrill; and now her hand did rise to her stomach. He's escaped us all. Mordred . . .

'Why haven't you got him?' she shouted, almost sorry that she had been incubating a death in there and not a new life. Time was tearing now, faster than she had ever known it, hurtling down from the hinterland, and the sea was baying louder, luring her away even as she faced the six.

None of them would speak. To Morgan the string of silent moments felt as long as a baby's full term.

'Tell me,' she shrieked, damned if she would be left with a dead man; corpses, after all, were these women's speciality. 'Why haven't you brought him out?'

'He will not come,' one called back, glancing from Morgan to the older woman and then back again, as if uncertain whether to show how well she spoke the language. 'Not with us. He refuses to go near the water.'

Morgan thought hard before saying anything.

For a moment she thought they were lying. Teasing. But at once she knew they were not. It was much more likely that they had known how to quicken him all along. Mordred . . . Not a merlin.

Morgan pictured him inside, sitting narrow-eyed on the couch now, his head low, his feet four-square on the red-tiled floor. For all his youth and unhardened hands, there was a definite sense of menace about him. She wasn't surprised that the women hadn't been able to bring him out. Possibly he had no reason to come.

'Is the villa his?' she asked, turning to the leader. 'Is this his home? Is that really what he's come back for?'

'He came for you,' said one of the younger six to her back. But the word 'for' sounded more like 'from'. Morgan shut her eyes. Time was roaring in her ears, urging her away towards the calling water.

She raised her wrap like an eagle's wings, then drew it more tightly around her. She opened her eyes and none of the women had moved. Mordred . . . They seemed to be blocking her way back to the villa. She couldn't go in to him . . . wouldn't even try. Not yet. The water wanted her more.

Silently she stepped over the 'A' that she had made in the dust, then passed the old woman and made for the cliff path. She was down on the shore almost before she knew it. Her feet seemed not to be touching the ground.

'Anna!' she called as she passed through the merlins' graveyard.

She wanted to hold the girl's hand, hug her, hide for a little while behind her tininess. But Anna didn't come, however often Morgan cried for her.

Her voice seemed to be swallowed by the sea. The tide was well in. Morgan picked her way over the rocks which now marked the water-margin. She had no idea if the women were watching from above, and she didn't look to see. Back in the cliff's shadows she thought she could glimpse other figures flitting: male, long-haired, leathery will-o'-the-wisps.

A late breeze blew. A first rogue wave seeped over her feet. The water was still warm from the day's heat. Summer Country heat. Morgan splashed on, closer to the far headland than she had ever been before. There were no lights, no smoke, no torches. Just time and heat and this huge onrushing ocean. *You have done what you thought was right* . . . And she had. She had.

'Anna!' she called into the night, more plaintively now. 'Anna! . . .'

She kept glancing from side to side. It felt as if the sea were as high to her left as the soaring cliff was to her right. She couldn't tell how it had suddenly steepened, but the waves' foam-flecks appeared to be towering over her.

The sea, the cliff and the two headlands were forming an enormous cauldron. The ultimate dumping-ground of all the time that rolled down from behind the villa. Here time could go in and out at will, twist itself into new shapes and patterns. She could believe, now, that this was the place where all things began and ended, where everything finally turned into itself.

Your condition . . . She put both hands to her stomach, felt the swelling and began to shrink bodily around it.

'Anna?' she breathed, turning from the water. As she turned, she lost her footing and fell.

Still holding her stomach, she didn't even try to break her fall. Her head hit a rock, but she didn't black out at once. Much later she remembered smiling as she lay prone and thinking, Now it's my turn to sleep. Now I can let time carry me on . . .

She felt this new fast time eddying over her like an army of ants, darker than the darkness, deeper into the cauldron. Water lapped at her, over her. She never doubted that someone would come to save her.

Still she smiled as she sank into the rock, closing her eyes on the swarming black march: time like a single stream of merlins' hair, wave after wave after wave. *Your condition* . . . She was confident. She knew from what the

74

woman had said that there was more to be saved than just herself.

A shape arose from the darkness: not distant but dim. It massed before Morgan's closed eyes just as the women's barge had once dissolved. Partly like a wave, yet partly like a person. It looked close enough to touch but its fingers soughed through her own once, twice, three times.

'Logres is coming,' whispered the water as it entered her, and in that moment the water *was* all the women. 'Through you, Logres will come . . .'

Hours passed between the two promises. Time tore on, immersing Morgan then raising her up. Hands held her, pressed her down – not on to the rock but into a couch.

She knew she was back in the villa now. Back in the pool room. She had surfaced in the room through the pool. Hands played under her waist, cleaning her, brisk but not unpleasant. Fingers probed her mouth, parting her lips for fluid food. Meal after meal after meal. She let herself drift, and the hands felt like her own: a second pair bursting out to tend her in this suspension.

For so long the hours in this Avalon had oozed by sluggishly. Here now was their other face: storming past as if undammed, balancing out the great slowness of before. Months flew by; seasons cycled. Real time too, as real as any that Morgan had ever lived through. And in part – she felt sure – she was making this happen, the part of her that was Fay, that took her power to the water and caused all these reactions.

Often she didn't know if the hands were reaching out of her or in. Mostly the fingers sifted her guts, painlessly promising hurts. Sifting, searching, testing, inspecting.

'Logres . . .' she heard again and again. Slowly it started to make a sort of sense. It sounded to Morgan like a garden, a billowing bright new Eden. A land of promise arising from the water.

The hands moved on inside her – soothing her pains, not causing them. She knew that she was incubating again; she had to be. That was why she had come into Avalon: to be with the sleeper, to do what she knew to be right, helping her at last to turn into her truest self . . .

The couch was afloat. The water heaved beneath her, roiling with heat from the fires deep inside. She curled up tight, protecting her cargo.

The hands were speaking, tapping out the truth. She wanted this new voyage to go on for ever. The fingers flexed faster, but Morgan felt so full. Scarcely room for the hands to move. Out they came to smooth her surface. A second chance, and not for her alone. The start of the Great Remaking.

Wake now, coaxed the fingers. *Wake and make Logres . . .*

But Morgan didn't want to wake. She curled herself tighter, made herself smaller. Too small for more than one hand to grab her. She felt so young: bloodied, fresh from out of her mother. One infant among a holdful, but all the rest were dead.

She tried to burrow deeper into the cold flesh around her. An infant with an older mind, a child that had to hide. But she couldn't move, couldn't shift amid this skin and bone. And she knew each of the dead girls. Every one was her, the powerless babies she could have been, the seeds of the weaker women she could have become. Then the hand closed on her.

She made to kick, to bite and scratch. But as it hauled her up, away from all her aborted selves, she grew back into herself inside its grip. It held her between her legs, its fingertips intruding. *You will have everything you need . . .*

It pulled her up through her own surface and set her down and then was gone.

Morgan opened her eyes. She was in her own sleeping quarters at the villa.

Sunlight crept in through the doorway behind her. Her hand was between her legs, her wrist bent at an unnatural angle. She lay on her side, in a rucked-up green gown, facing the long wall mirror.

The clamour of the hands slowly faded in her head. Outside all was quiet. And in here there was no one. Only herself and her own head-to-knee reflection in the mirror.

She saw her own image clear-eyed, recognized her new, true self. She saw too why her wrist felt odd. Her arm didn't extend directly to her crotch, but followed the contour of her hugely-swollen stomach. She pushed her fingers under the gown and over the great mound. *Your condition . . .* The baby looked almost ready to be born.

Part Two

AIR

SIX

Stupefied, for two days Morgan left her room only to use the latrine.

She didn't sleep, couldn't eat, barely dared to breathe for fear of missing a telltale sound somewhere else in the villa. He had to be close by. Mordred . . . Deep in the nights she could almost taste his smoky smell. But she never saw a trace of him. And all she ever heard was the beating of the sea, the bleating of the gulls.

For hours she stood exposing herself in the long mirror. She had thought she had been rising up through the ruins of herself. Now she knew that she had just been reconstructing the rubble. Often she cried, but the silent tears seemed to belong only to her reflection. So did her swelling. It looked different from the way it had looked in her first pregnancy, the line running down from her navel was fainter. And her load seemed higher up now, nestling just below her breasts, both blue-vein-bulbous again.

Her legs and arms had thickened too. The armlet was biting so deep into her shoulder that she couldn't have moved it up or down. With its gaping mouth and single eye, the dead king's gift seemed to leer back at her from the glass, as if it had won some personal, irreversible victory.

Don't think, she told herself over and over. She knew from before that her mind could take her only so far. And with every passing moment, she shrank deeper inside the bloated body that now held her captive.

After two days the sea's tone seemed to change. Mournful but menacing too. The new noise made her think of merlins. Of the eerie crowd-sounds she used to hear from packed halls when the long-haired liars came to entertain. In the end it nauseated her so much that she uprooted herself from her room and tried to escape it in the villa's hinterland.

Outside, the season hadn't changed. The rising ground was as glitteringly sea-green as before. Apples still weighed down the trees in the orchard. The stain on the statue still looked wet. *Don't think . . .* Down in the water she must have slipped through a fold in time. Her world had turned inside out like a sail hit by a sudden cross-wind. But only her own world. And now it had changed back.

She didn't go far inland. The song from the shore seemed to follow her, and the apple-orchard's gradient wasn't so easy for her now. After half a mile her calves screamed for her to stop, and her thin gown was soaked through with sweat. But she went out again the next day – heaving herself around the hinterland in a new beating of the bounds, asserting her own right, reclaiming what had never really been hers in the first place.

The skyline above was better defined now. Twice Morgan thought she saw movement up there. Dark men circling slowly, as if they had been conjured up out of the ridge's oceanic earth. None looked like the man called Mordred. The man who had refused to go near the sea.

Early the next morning, after a third wakeful night, Morgan left the villa for the cliff-top. Her big letter 'A' still lay sharp in the forecourt's dust. There was no wind, no sound but that of ordinary waves.

Before reaching the head of the path, she thought she glimpsed a barge near the white horizon. Birds came winging in. Not gulls. Bigger, blacker. Scorching in formation across the lower sky, making for the nearer headland.

The shore below was deserted save for two figures. For a moment, appalled, she presumed that the one further up was her man. But it was only a merlin. Dead, unburied, the air above him grey with flies.

Unlike the merlins that Morgan had seen here before, this one gave every sign of having been killed where he lay, just above the high tide-line. His head and neck were dark with blood. A similarly-darkened rock sat on the sand close by.

The only other person in view was Anna, directly beneath Morgan's feet.

She was skipping around a little heap of stones among the tide pools. Her feet seemed barely to be touching the sand. Occasionally she would pause, squat, rearrange the stones, then dance on. There were flashes as the morning sun glinted on something shiny. A line of pearly shells perhaps. Morgan watched mesmerized, gladly distracted from the one body decaying on the sand and the other growing so fast inside her.

She watched Anna's antics for a while longer, then gingerly went down. Near the foot of the path, she noticed streaks of red on the girl's billowing blue shift. There were stains too on the sand, close to where she had now heaped the stones into a little pyramid-shaped cairn.

Morgan's step faltered. Anna hadn't seen her yet. She could still have pulled away, gone back to the villa; but nervously she went on.

Anna looked up, showing no surprise at Morgan's new shape. But as Morgan stepped on to the sand, she became self-conscious. With in-turned lips, she flopped beside her cairn and busily readjusted the stones all over again. This time, Morgan thought, she was possibly trying to hide something.

'Hello,' she called to the kneeling girl. 'What have you done to yourself?' She waved an arm in front of her to indicate the smeared shift.

'Nothing,' Anna answered, eyes down, fiddling with the stones.

'It looks like blood on you,' said Morgan, slowing to avoid the dark on the sand, then stopping in front of the cairn.

'No,' Anna said quickly. She glanced up, and raised a hand as if to protect the left side of her head.

84

Morgan smiled, perplexed. She flexed her toes in her sandals. The marks on the girl's clothing looked fresh, perhaps not even dry. She pictured open wounds on her scrawny flesh under the material; remembered the heaped-up body a hundred paces away. *Don't think* . . .

Morgan stepped closer, searching the child for a sign of ageing since last she had seen her. Anna kept her hand up at her left brow, as if to shield her eyes from the sun. But the sun was right behind her. And the girl wasn't a moment older than before. Morgan quailed to think of her own child staying for ever foetal, of herself perpetually pregnant.

She looked away to the shadows under the cliff, where she had fancied that she saw moving merlins just before her fall. Her eyes were drawn back to the dead man. Briefly the dirge soughed through the air around her.

Anna, as if alerted, clambered to her feet. The sound was different again now. Like the tolling of a bell. Loud, insistent. Not the sort of ringing that had once warned Arthur's people of yet another Sea Wolf raid. This was more resigned. Not so much a warning of what was to come as a commiseration with what had already begun.

Morgan pointed at the merlin when the din subsided. 'Why is he still there? Why hasn't he been buried like the rest?'

Anna bit on her hair. 'Because the other man killed him.'

'The man from the villa?' Mordred . . . She couldn't yet say his name.

Anna nodded.

'Why?'

'They were talking.' She glanced away. 'About you. What you are.' Her eyelashes fluttered. 'What', Morgan noticed, not 'who'. Sister, mistress; sister, mistress . . . 'And then the man killed him. With a rock on his head.'

'When?'

'The day you went in the water.'

'How do you know they were talking about me?'

'I was close. I heard.'

'About the baby? Was it about that?' Morgan knew it must have been. About the seed he had sown in his dreams.

Anna shrugged. Morgan stared at her hard. She wanted to squat or kneel in front of her so that their eyes could be level, but in her current state the manoeuvre would have been too difficult. Instead she offered her hand. The girl took it; her fingers felt like twigs. She stared expressionlessly at Morgan's stomach.

'It will be a boy again,' she said flatly.

'You think so?' Morgan swallowed. She herself had no instinct about what she was carrying. It could have been a swaddled stone pushed up inside her. It could have been thin air; not once had she felt a tremor of life. All she knew was that it was hers; that it had been planned for her in advance, and that something very large now depended on its birth.

'At least this time,' Anna went on, 'it is not your brother's.'

She spat out the last word and Morgan glared at her,

startled. 'My brother is dead,' she reminded the girl, tightening her grip on the small hand. 'And besides, I thought you didn't believe in him.'

Anna said nothing. Morgan looked out over the water. The barge appeared again, closer to the shore, only to be obscured by a rising wave. *The others and I mark out the boundaries . . .* Morgan's talk with Moronoe now seemed so remote: all those allusions to second chances, new kingdoms, Great Remakings.

'What do they do on that barge?' she asked. 'Fish?'

Anna shrugged again, pulling her hand away. This question seemed to trouble her more than the others.

'Don't you ever go out on it yourself?'

'No.' Her top lip was trembling. But Morgan wouldn't let this drop.

'Why is that?'

'It is not time.' She smiled out of the side of her mouth, but Morgan had never seen a less amused child. She looked at her harder. This girl was so like Guenever. Apparently open, never quite fully what she seemed. Skidding about beneath her skin. A muted kind of rival. But over what? Over whom?

'Tell me,' Morgan said. 'It is blood on you, isn't it?'

'Yes,' the girl shot back with a grin. 'But not *my* blood!'

'Whose, then?'

Anna returned her hand to her temple. 'It was on the knife. I wiped it.'

'What knife?' Morgan struggled down on to one knee. It saved her from shouting into the fresh sea breeze.

But Anna knelt too. She pressed her lips against her higher knee, which was protruding through a rip in the shift. She seemed to be sulking. Morgan wasn't sure why this mattered so much, to both of them. And she could still in that moment have stood and walked away. No one was saying that she had to stay.

'What knife?' Morgan repeated.

'I found it over there,' she muttered at her leg, jerking her head towards the tide. 'There was blood on it and I wiped it on me, but it kept on bleeding.'

Morgan swallowed. Looking down, she saw a scatter of bone needles. Had the knife been washed in the water or left there by the women? Had Anna been involved in killing the merlin? All the merlins? Her heart beat faster. *It kept on bleeding* . . . 'Can you show it to me?'

Anna's lips were glued to her knee, but still she managed to shake her head. Morgan reached out over the cairn and stroked her tangled hair. 'Show it to me,' she said. 'Why are you hiding it? . . .'

Anna glanced at the stones. Morgan thought she understood. The look was surely deliberate . . . an invitation. She thought so even afterwards. Anna genuinely wanted Morgan to push over the cairn and take out what was inside it. And so she smiled and began to extend her arm.

What happened next seemed to have no sequence. Cause sheared away from effect. Suddenly there was a flurry of hands. Her own and little Anna's, with fresh blood already spattering them. Not her blood . . . Not the girl's . . .

Maybe for a moment Anna tried to grip her wrist to stop her from touching the stones. Maybe she cried out in protest. Again, Morgan could recall only the louder shout of pain and fear: a recollection steeped in guilt, because whatever had happened had surely had its origin in her, in that power which – undisciplined – would at random spill out and run amok.

And then among the hands there was the uncovered knife. Not *in* her hand or Anna's but among them, almost like a fifth hand itself; apparently moving too. Plain enough to look at. Old – a bit of bone and rusted metal – its hilt wrapped with skin and two brass studs inserted for a grip.

The red on the blade wasn't rust. As soon as it rose between them it was dripping. Morgan's own hands were immediately sticky. Both she and Anna seemed to be holding it, tugging, wrenching, neither letting go. But the handle was barely big enough for one hand. Morgan's hand.

She couldn't possibly have thrust it up. Even with Anna standing now on the scattered stones and pulling, Morgan on her knees could not have lunged with it. She wouldn't have wanted to. All her effort was going into dragging it back the other way. Yet the knife entered Anna's face before the girl lost her balance and started to topple forward.

Only after this did Morgan remember her falling, drenched in the shower of new blood, and that shout. A shout which seemed to echo across the water at them both. And although Morgan let go of the handle at once, the blade seemed to sink in further as she fell.

The rest was burned on Morgan's memory. The knife came free as the girl hit the ground face-down. She didn't move. Her arms were spread, her knees drawn up, her squirrel hair fanned out around her.

Morgan, whimpering, backed along the sand on her haunches like an ape. She was sure that the knife had pierced her eye, and then gone deeper still. It had seemed to meet no resistance, as if the girl were two-dimensional. But she had blood inside her. The scuffed-up sand was black with it; so was the sand around the knife. The knife that had bled before it struck home.

Morgan couldn't move, couldn't cry. Her breath made tiny gull-squeals in the back of her throat. Her face felt full of a hideous stench – vegetal, a smell of well-advanced decay.

The stain around the knife looked deeper now than the stain by the girl's prone head. She thought she would never move on from this moment. She would stay on the shore for the rest of time, gazing at the new corpse that she didn't dare approach.

Then she smelled smoke, hot on the air like some beast's spoor.

She didn't hear or see him come. He sank to his knees beside Anna as if he had dropped down from the sky. He turned the girl over with her face away from Morgan. His own face was impassive under the stubby crop that Morgan herself had given him. His eyes were hooded.

His nose twitched, as if he had smelled something even worse than he had just seen.

He didn't flinch as he looked, touched, wetted his fingertips and started to clean.

Morgan watched, but couldn't really see him through her panic. He was too close. There in his grey tunic, a great dark-pale blur. It seemed impossible that he was beside her. He didn't belong; not in this animated way. The world must have turned itself inside out again to let him through.

The breeze gusted between Morgan and the two of them. It ruffled Anna's shift, giving the impression that she was stirring. Slowly Morgan came back into line with herself, and found that she could be silent and stand.

Still Anna's face was hidden, her head cradled in his arm as he worked at the wound. Once he glanced past her at the knife on the sand. It was as if he were keeping an eye on it, like a dog he didn't trust.

It had been more than just the wind inside Anna's shift. Morgan saw her foot move, then her hand come up to her hair. Sighing, she closed her eyes and touched her stomach.

'She'll live,' he said, sounding as mournful as the song that had driven Morgan from the villa. And his voice was so deep that it seemed to echo in his throat.

Anna turned her face a little way towards Morgan. Her eyes were open. Both eyes. Her forehead was pink from the cleaned blood. A jagged cut ran along her hairline. Livid, serpentine, but already unbleeding.

Morgan wondered how much Mordred had seen of

their scuffle; she wondered how much that mattered. He was sniffing hard now, jerking back his head each time. Was he possibly smelling the blood? Morgan asked herself. Was it the scent of blood that had lured him out into the open?

Anna stared at her unaccusingly, and apparently un-shocked. She fitted so snugly into the crook of his arm. Her wide eyes seemed to be saying, He holds me, but he's never held you.

Morgan tried to smile. She couldn't control her breathing. His active, animal nearness dizzied her, her head was full of his smoky smell. And she was shivering, as if he were still radiating cold, like some dark, inverted sun. She wished he would look at her. If only he would look at her, and tell her what *he* knew about all this madness around them.

He straightened himself and gently put Anna on her own two feet.

The child stood between them, gashed and swaying, like a tiny arbiter between two reluctant wrestlers. Then Mordred stepped away to where the knife lay and squatted over it.

'She said she found it,' Morgan called hoarsely to his long curved back. She had to say something. 'She said it came in on the tide . . .'

He didn't answer. His silence raked at her. She felt as if he were making her do a kind of penance there in front of them both. *I did nothing wrong* . . . she wanted to scream, as so often before. *I'm not to blame* . . .

Finally he poked out a finger and smeared the blood

from the blade. Then he flicked it over and similarly cleaned the other side. He stared out to sea before picking it up and stashing it absently in his belt. When he stood and turned, his downcast face looked more drawn, his skin more pallid.

'It's mine,' he said in the direction of Morgan's distended stomach. 'It followed me here.' Like a dog, thought Morgan.

He frowned deeply. His face was unreadable beneath those sorry jet-black tufts. Anna, she noticed, had made no move to claim the knife for herself, the knife for which she had fought Morgan so fiercely. It crossed Morgan's mind that she might actually have been keeping it for him.

Then he startled her by speaking. 'The girl,' he said slowly to the sand, as if they had now been left alone together, 'her name is Anna?'

'Yes? Don't you . . . Do you know her?'

'Not like that,' he murmured, gesturing at the girl with one hand while grasping for hair at his shoulder. In his distraction, he had clearly forgotten that he had been scalped. 'Nothing like that . . .'

Anna herself said nothing. Mordred just dipped his head and swallowed. Show me your eyes, Morgan pleaded inside herself. Show me your eyes . . . But instead he turned aside, his great nostrils flaring. 'You didn't go into the water when you came here?' he breathed, like a man talking in his sleep. 'You weren't immersed? That merlin told me you just walked ashore.'

'Me? Yes, I did. But what of it?'

93

Seeming not to hear her, he walked away towards his own flyblown victim.

Morgan's shivers became more violent. She held herself tightly where she stood, watching Mordred pass the corpse and wander on towards the headland.

Only as he moved further away did his shape at last start to make sense to her. At first, shockingly, he reminded her of her brother. It was all in the set of his shoulders. Whatever the weather, Arthur had always walked in this same way: head back, neck stiff, eyes wide, daring the elements to affect him.

And Mordred now seemed to be making the same silent challenge. Taunting the water, setting himself against the mists and the rising sun. But he wasn't Arthur. And the longer Morgan looked, the less he seemed to be swaggering. He was young, bemused, still turning into himself. Not Arthur, never Arthur . . .

Anna wafted past her in the opposite direction. Morgan twisted around to find the barge becalmed in the distant shallows and all seven women coming ashore.

Anna went to them and disappeared inside their huddle. Morgan felt pity for the child, but no real remorse. Nothing was simple. She had felt a grisly kind of triumph in drawing her blood – just like she had felt on handing over her own first child. That same sickening secret surge, the dark empowering confidence that nothing was beyond her – no trick, no feat, no aspect of catastrophe.

Morgan waited for a while, staring at the smeary stones from Anna's spilled pile. The sun burned hot on her back.

Her baby felt icy in her belly. Why had Mordred refused to look at her? It had to be revulsion, because he knew what everyone else knew. *What you are . . .* That she had been her own brother's lover.

The ghostly sound was welling again on the breeze. It seemed to be centred on the dead man, playing him like an instrument. Hushed and guttural; male but not quite human. Morgan didn't look at the body before hobbling back up the cliff-path. It felt like the least of what she was leaving behind.

Once inside the villa, she couldn't get the knife out of her mind. All day she waited for the sound of Mordred's footsteps – in hope now rather than dread. Any vestige of self-sufficiency had left her. She felt helpless, incompetent, unbearably alone. But he didn't come.

Before she turned in for the night, she undressed and stood trembling in front of her mirror. An almost visible new quality hedged her image. An uncertainty of line; a shadow thrown by no light and on to no hard surface. Suddenly she thought poor little Anna's eyes were staring back out of the glass at her. The next moment, though, they were Guenever's.

Guenever: so calm there at the first child's birth. *It's not your son . . .* The womb had been Morgan's, but never the child. And who was she growing this new baby for? Who would be waiting to take it? Not once had she thought she might keep it. Not once had she thought she might want to.

The eyes once again were her own. But when she ran her hands over her upper body, the touch felt unfamiliar.

95

She looked away, kept moving her hands, but never as far as her swelling. Then she wept. Only then. And not just for Anna. I'm afraid of this baby, she sobbed to herself, afraid, afraid . . .

She stepped right up to the mirror, pushed her wet cheek against it, licked it, clawed at her own raking hands behind the glass, turned to press her thigh and breast against the flat, smudged coolness.

It wasn't any kind of communion with herself but she had to go on. Someone had to touch her. It could have been anyone. The corpse down on the shore, even.

Hard against the glass she started to laugh. Tear-choked giggles, a woman at the edge of herself. A woman who could never seem to get any closer.

She sank to the floor, stunned by the imminence of so much new life when all she felt around her was the threat of blood and death.

SEVEN

Morgan was running.

All that night her dreams had been appalling. Dreams of Anna drowning in blood. Dreams of the knife leaping up to stab at Mordred's eyes and throat and groin. Of Morgan herself pushing the blade very slowly into her own bloated torso. And through them all, the wind-blown sea had been calling to her: 'Logres, Logres, Logres . . .'

But now there was silence. And Morgan was on her feet, moving as fast as she could with the child inside her. Out on to the villa's forecourt, breathless towards the cliff-top. This, bizarrely, was the worst dream of all. No blood in it, no knives. Just a fear that the sea had disappeared – gone for ever, revealing a soundless hell: deserts in flames now instead of a sea-bed, a whole people burning . . .

No, Morgan whimpered. No, bring the sea back! Her eyes stung with dryness, her throat ached from parching.

The heat was intolerable there at the cliff's edge. *No!* she screamed louder. The fire drew her nearer: she saw the flesh frying. No! she screamed, hoarse, before taking the last step.

'*No!* Stop! Don't! Get back! . . .'

The shouts from below woke her up in her night-clothes.

Dawn had broken, though the night mists still hung heavy. Morgan was standing, bent-kneed and tremulous, just a yard from the cliff-top. Ahead of her the sea came surging in. For the first time in her life she had sleepwalked.

'Go back! Back!'

The male voice beneath her was stunningly real. She lowered her eyes, but only when he moved did Morgan see him in his wraith-grey tunic. Mordred, approaching from the other headland now. He paused, their eyes met.

Morgan gripped her armlet. It was as if she were seeing him after years of absence, not just a matter of hours. The sight of his eyes altered everything. Glazed, long-lashed, searching, they gave his quiet beauty an entirely new depth. His drowsy gaze wouldn't move from her face. And then Morgan thought that she saw in them, to her infinite relief, a need that reflected her own.

His arms hung by his sides. He had saved her. Him. Suddenly composed, Morgan smiled down. It was as if they were standing on the same level. He seemed to have scaled himself up so that their eyes could meet. She felt that she could have put out a hand and been within his range. He continued simply to stare until in the end she had to look away herself – to the sand, the sky, the distant headland.

Her movement seemed to release him. He set off again up the shore, passing the merlin's corpse without looking down at it. *The other man killed him . . . With a rock . . . About you . . .*

He kept on glancing at the water. But Morgan guessed that he saw little of the world around him. That his soul and senses were still in transit even if his body was so solidly, sturdily here. But she took comfort from what she had seen in his eyes. When the baby came, he would surely be with her. This time like the last, she wouldn't have to be alone.

Farther up the shore, the women's torches burned. Morgan smelled them before she saw their thin smoke against the daylight. Then suddenly she saw Mordred wrench himself around towards the cliff. He sprang forward, his arms poised as if he were about to rush at some merlin's corpse that had risen outside Morgan's vision.

There was a little strangled shriek. Mordred shook his fist, turned away, then strode on faster. Morgan saw Anna scurrying over the stones, past the corpse to where the women waited by the water.

The incident puzzled Morgan, and made her feel less confident. She couldn't think how the girl had upset him, or why he had reacted so strongly.

Anna drifted between the women. Some of them were cooking on small fires. There was still so much that Morgan had to find out from them. But not, she thought, until she had spoken with Mordred. Not before she had heard his side.

It rained intermittently all that day. By evening Anna hadn't come to the villa with food, so Morgan went out to pick apples and berries. The rain then stopped, and the sun broke through just before setting.

Collecting the fruit exhausted her, but not in an unpleasant way. Propped against a tree to eat it, she day-dreamed that the shore below curved on to infinity. And behind each new headland, scenes similar to her own were being lived out. A million different Morgans, a queen for every inlet, a million different Mordreds slowly being woken.

Then she smelled smoke. Turning, she saw beacons burning high on the ridge, and a figure coming down fast towards the villa's cluster of outbuildings. Mordred.

He didn't look in her direction. Darkness had fallen; he probably wouldn't have seen her anyway. Morgan didn't call – she still wasn't sure of him, of how he might respond to her. Instead she eased herself up, taking what remained of her fruit, and went across to where he had gone.

There were workshops there, a granary, a disused tannery, the room with the loom. Morgan had looked around them all in her first days at the villa, but she had rarely been back since. The whole area stank of animal dirt. She'd seen rats too, and twice she had disturbed bats in the airless corners.

She found Mordred standing outside a ruined joinery. His back was to her, his head cocked. Suddenly he sank to his haunches and threw a wild look over his shoulder. If Morgan hadn't known better, she would have said that he had smelled her coming.

Newly confused, she stepped forward, close enough for them to speak. The huts were blocking out the beacons' light, so they could still barely see each other. Morgan held out the fruit to him, like a peace offering to a savage. She wished he would stand, smile, start at last to set her own mind at rest.

'Thank you for calling out this morning,' she began. 'It was a night-fright. I had no idea what I was doing . . .'

He frowned at her glassily, still crouched. He looked like a man lying in ambush for himself.

Morgan placed a hand on her big stomach. She meant it as a plea, not a challenge, to show him her own anxiety. The apples and berries cascaded to the ground between them. 'Will you come to the villa?' she asked him unsteadily.

Mordred gazed at her in a peculiar way — as if he wanted to sew her lips together, but with the needle clamped between his own perfect teeth. Without warning he stood. His head was tilted. He could have been tasting the night-air that swarmed around her, testing it to see if he could stay so close and survive. The merlin excelled himself here, Morgan thought; successfully steeped his mind in so much poison. Or was it something else? Was he simply mortified by what had happened in his sleep?

She peered into his dark, uncertain eyes, at his beard like a great blue-black bruise. At last he looked down.

He stared at his hand as if it were an exhibit – not so much a broken man as one put back together in a way that he simply didn't recognize from before.

We're alike, Morgan thought without quite knowing why. Two shouts in the same silence. But she knew that in this state he was beyond her. She lacked the energy to start telling him the truth about herself. And by saying the wrong thing now, she risked driving him away altogether. Soon she would need to be with him at any cost . . . but not yet. Not quite yet.

'You're welcome at the villa,' she said, making herself leave.

In the middle of the night she woke with a start. The air was so sour with smoke that she thought the villa must be on fire. And this was no dream.

Pulling on her wrap, she made first for the kitchens, then checked on each of the wings in turn. She found nothing, though the burning stench stayed strong. She pictured the women staking out torches all round the villa. But she told herself that it had to be coming from the beacons on the ridge.

Wide awake now, she made for the forecourt. Occasional ash flecks floated between the entrance pillars and over the chippings. But the smell was less oppressive in the open. Less smoky than damply steamy.

She leaned against the entrance arch and listened to the unfamiliar sound of gulls crying by night. The area in front of her was bathed in a rippling metallic blue light which was also unfamiliar. Morgan felt as if she were under water. As if in response to the air's burning, the villa's pool had swollen to take in the whole of the building, then spilled outside.

Soon the song from the shore started to rise. *Logres* . . . *Logres* . . .

Intrigued, Morgan found herself being drawn towards its source. She had never been out at this hour, when the tide was at its highest and all the corpses came through. The thought of it raked at her, but not enough to make her turn back. She needed to be in company, and if Mordred was still out of reach, she would have to make do with the women, or even little Anna.

The slurry of sound subsided as she neared the edge of the cliff. She closed her eyes and heard only the soft plash and purr of night-time water. Looking out, the horizon seemed both near and high. Almost on a level with herself. This was no conventional shore: not so much a place where earth met water as a kind of crucible where the two mysteriously meshed.

As if to bear this out, a boat appeared on the distant rim. Much larger than the barge, higher in the water, with multiple masts flying pennants. It could have been a galley, although Morgan saw no oars.

Heading from left to right, it seemed to be moving inside its own pale glow – as if the sea over there had risen so high that the moon was now shining directly behind it. Its course ran virtually parallel to Morgan's shore. Maybe, she thought, it was making for the bay beyond the headland.

But then it dipped abruptly, and for the length of a blink it disappeared.

It came back into view much lower against the wall of sea. Then for a longer stretch it vanished and returned lower still, while keeping to its rightward path. It looked for all the world to Morgan as if it were skidding down the water's face, not cutting a swathe across it. And even though it was passing closer now, it had stayed the same size as before.

Finally it disappeared a third time and didn't re-emerge. The glow faded gently afterwards, but first it dispersed itself over the surface – in the rough shape of a cross. Morgan, dizzied, let her eyes fall.

Planted torches were burning at the tideline, just down from where the murdered merlin lay. Morgan stepped closer to the edge.

A barge bobbed in the shallows. Moving fast in the dark, the women appeared to be loading it with stones from the cairns. Anna was running to and fro among them. She held a length of seaweed, trailing it behind her this time, not swatting. She looked out of sorts, unhappy. She might even have been whimpering under the gulls' cries.

The girl raced slower and slower. Then she threw down the seaweed, raised her arms in front of the nearest woman, and let herself be carried out to the barge.

'No!' Morgan cried, lifting one arm.

None of the heads turned.

'No!' Morgan shouted louder. 'Stay!'

The words blew back at her like spit on the wind. The

woman holding Anna waded on. The child was facing the cliff, but Morgan couldn't see if her eyes were raised or not. She rubbed at the armlet in frustration.

She couldn't risk going down – she might have been unable to hoist herself back up again – but she didn't want Anna to leave. The girl had seemed uneasy about the water before; Morgan couldn't believe that she was going willingly now. Worse, this felt like a response to their own dreadful tangle on the sand. Or even to Mordred's crazy shaking of his fist.

'*Don't!*' Morgan yelled.

The woman thigh-deep in the sea looked up. She must have been able to hear all along. And even at so great a distance Morgan knew that she was smiling.

Anna looked no bigger than a speck of blown dandelion in the barge. She was curled into the tightest ball, her head between her knees. Perhaps she was already feeling sick at what was about to happen.

Morgan badly wished she had been able to speak with her. To ask questions as much as to apologize. She watched breathlessly as the women climbed aboard the barge and cast off. There was something so final about it.

The smoke from the beacons far behind had reached here now. Men's smoke, surely. The men were closing in; the women moving out. Morgan felt marooned, the last of her kind.

The barge left its moorings at speed. The seven had abandoned their torches, but the cairn stones seemed to shine in the hold. Soon the smaller vessel was winking through the water like the galley from before. Vanish, appear, vanish, appear – as it were defying nature's law and scaling the sheer sea-wall.

Morgan shrank inside her wrap. The sound swelled again in the great bowl at her feet. Rising from the unmarked graves, mingling with the wind and smoke. Spiralling around her like a dense acoustic coat. *Logres, Logres . . .*

Then she saw the galley again. Nearer to the rim than the oncoming barge, but flickering now, and about to converge with it. Morgan gasped. The two became one: moonglow and stoneshine. Another bright cross-shape striped the water – and they were gone.

She clutched at her stomach; the noise grew softer. She shut her eyes tightly and clearly saw Guenever: momentous beside her at the first baby's birth, so selfless and caring. She thought she heard movement below in the scrub. Hustling, unearthly. Her eye fell on the murdered 'Land Man'. Killed for her, the girl had said. But who now was going to bury the body?

She tossed her head, badly vexed. She couldn't be alone. Not so close to her term. Guenever had helped her before; Guenever had cut the cord. This time it would have to be Mordred. There was simply no one else.

And he had to understand that. She had to make him see, in the best way she knew how.

She found him in the joinery, down among the fearsome dreck – his curved back exposed by the light of a lantern she had brought from the villa; curled on a carpet of hessian and hay, his head pressed to the wall.

Sharp spits of rain arrowed in on the new breeze. It didn't smell like wood burning. Fattier, greasier, much more pungent. Before going in, Morgan raised her eyes and saw the two great ridge fires. Wide apart but coming closer. A broken red horizon as high now as the sea.

'Mordred . . .' she choked at the shape on the floor. The syllables snagged at her, the name itself ate at her. She couldn't imagine any woman giving it to a newborn child. 'Now. We should be together now . . .'

She set down the lantern in the splintered doorway. Its beam picked out no more than the backs of his raised legs. 'Please, it's our child. Yours and mine. I can't be alone. Not now that the women have gone . . .'

She checked herself, knowing that already she had said more than she had intended. The words should have come after. She had to show him, not tell him. Touch, not talk. Then he would never be able to leave her.

Morgan stepped inside, breathing through her mouth against the fetor. He hadn't flinched once since she had come. She went to him and knelt in the hessian, glad that it was so dark. He could have been anyone. Anyone she liked.

She touched his haunch and was awed by the coldness through the cloth. He was no warmer now than he had been while in the villa. She fanned out her fingers; he could have been marble.

'The women haven't gone,' rumbled up from the

mournful depths of him. It was like hearing the subsoil speak. 'There's nowhere to go . . .'

'Don't talk now,' Morgan soothed him, running her hand higher. She saw again those two sea-vessels, winking on their collision course.

'There's nowhere else,' he maundered on, 'let me tell you . . .'

'No, no, no.' Morgan shifted herself sidelong to him, ran her hand up into his hair, against its stubbly grain. Gently she took a handful and tried to ease his head around to face her.

'Let me tell you . . .' he gasped again as he let himself be turned.

'Don't speak, my sweet. You don't have to speak.' She kneaded his arm, strong and spare in its sleeve, then lowered her lips on to his. She was with him. Alike. Two shouts in the same dark silence.

His kiss was tender but dry. His tongue lashed inside her mouth, but as if it wanted to get out, not reach deeper. She had known that he would need to be led; she had known and was ready.

Still sidelong to him, Morgan put her hands to his head, clamping him, and snaked her tongue around his. She wanted him wetter; wanted him to float in his own wetness. He needed that. But not as much as she did. *Nowhere else*, he had rambled at her. It was true. This, for them, was the only place.

She slewed him around bodily. He was fighting, but not against her. She kissed his hair, shifting on to her back to keep any pressure off the child. He shook his head, wedged tight against her shoulder, already rooting.

Deftly she reached up to slide back her wrap, unfastened her gown and freed her breasts. She didn't need sex herself. Not here, not now. Maybe she never had. Nothing was simple, least of all this. Sex was just the length to which she was prepared to go. Playing with fire perhaps, but by now she had learned how to deal with the flames.

Great shudders racked him. His teeth touched her nipple and she felt his hand claw at the hem of her gown. His fingers came fast up her leg, as if they were running away from themselves.

Morgan lay still for him. She had to be his sleeper here, just as he had once been hers. But first she reached down and tore away her undergarment. His wrist sat shaggy between her white thighs. She kissed his head one last time, then turned on to her side.

His fingers slid high inside her from behind. She waited for the rest of him, prepared to raise her rump. *Bull, bear, goat, ram* . . . But his hand just kept working, two fingers inside her, then three. His touch was frostily cautious, but not because of her. He had hit his own limits, mumbling and grunting with nothing like lust.

He kept her at arm's length, touching her nowhere else. She shut her wet eyes and made herself his sleeper. But still he only handled her – and then she understood.

It was the child. His child, theirs, just beyond his reach. He was talking to the foetus with his slowly-flexing fingers. Sign language inside her.

Morgan moaned. 'You can put yourself inside me . . .' She reached behind to grip his stiffened arm. 'The baby will be safe. You can have all you want . . .'

All you want. All you need. He dragged out his hand and, stuttering in torment, put Morgan on her back and pushed apart her thighs. Then his head was down between them. He still hadn't touched her stomach. All he needed was inside.

His tongue, teeth and beard took over from his fingers. Morgan stared into the blackness above, confused but content. He gnawed at her wet flesh, licked and chewed its flimsy folds, but only for the child.

The baby will be safe . . . It was stronger than either of them. Already it had escaped both its makers. Bigger than them, bigger than this island and everything in it, arching over all like a sky beneath the sky.

Suddenly, in spite of herself, Morgan came. A single empty judder.

She shivered back to stillness, gripping his hair like handles, then tore him off and pressed her own hands between her legs. She felt so far away, like the third person involved in what had just happened. A very poor third.

For some moments she lay against him. He was silent now, motionless and cold – like Anna when they had lain so close on the couch. But Morgan needed more. She couldn't be bypassed; more had to happen. This fire had started to burn her too. She couldn't, after all, stay asleep.

She grabbed his wrist and kissed his forearm, then his

inner elbow. *Everything you need . . .* I can't be alone! she screamed inside.

Using him to drag herself up, she pressed him back and thrust both hands under his tunic. The loincloth tore, he sprang out hard.

'Now,' she told him, launching her great bulk higher up his body, pinning him with her naked knees. Against the cap of one she felt something cold, which she guessed was that awful knife's handle. 'Now, because we have to . . . Forget who I am. I could be anyone . . .'

His flesh was as cold as the merlins' on the shore. Morgan sat forward to feed him up inside her, then sank down on the length of him. Her shin touched the knife as she started to rock.

He reared up close to the baby. Soothing it, not threatening. She had wanted him to have her in the same way as her brother. But this wasn't Arthur. The king had tried to kill when he crammed himself in; Mordred kept the baby safe.

But hard though he stayed, this didn't feel right. He seemed to be the wrong man inside her. Not like it had been on the poolside couch; this had no grand momentum. She almost wished he would prise her off. But now he was helpless beneath her. Stop me, stop me, she prayed as she moved herself. Then it happened.

This time the knife's blade caught her, and she yelped at the smart. But when she looked down, the blood was on Mordred. A great fat scratch on his chest in the dimness. Another ran across his cheek. A third had striped his shoulder.

Morgan recoiled. Further lesions marked him as she gasped. His head beat from side to side, his eyes open wide but showing only white.

'Mordred! . . .' she cried, afraid – but just for him.

She slid herself off and tried to calm him down. His body was a barrier as he lay there fenced off by his own skin and bone. And when she looked closer, his skin was spotless. His eyes had come back, but looked dead in his head. She stared deeply into them, and saw their life return for her.

Then she pushed herself up and got to her feet. There was no sign of blood, on him or on her. The knife – she now noticed – was nowhere near. It lay on a low ledge in the wall. Its blade had been wrapped round with muslin.

No blade, no blood – not this time. Maybe, she told herself, she had needed a reason to stop. Needed it so badly that she had conjured the illusion; even if in truth it had been less of an illusion than a promise of what was to come: her own infallible vision of the hurts that lay in store.

But she had brought him far enough. He wouldn't leave her now. She didn't even have to stay in this vile place to be sure of that.

Mordred turned and curled himself tight. The fingers of one hand were in his mouth and ear, those of the other in the crack between his buttocks. He seemed to be trying to plug himself up, to stop any hand from reaching in too deep. But Morgan now knew he was hers for the asking.

She backed to where she had left the lantern. In the doorway she rearranged her gown and wrap before leaving for the villa. She wasn't going to be alone. When the time came, she would know where to find him.

EIGHT

The baby didn't start that night, though Morgan hauled herself from room to room, desperate to bring it on. It felt too large to be inside her still. In a sense it no longer was – not all of it. Down on that filthy hut's floor, it had begun to seep out of her like air and spread around them both.

Waiting, waiting, waiting . . . Again and again the next day her thoughts curved back to the corpse on the shore. Beaten by the endless wheels of rain, left behind by the women – as if for Morgan to deal with herself.

By late afternoon the rain at last relented. The child was no nearer and Morgan surged with energy. Feeling capable of anything to make the baby come quicker, she stepped outside into smoky sunlight. She didn't know if the darkness above meant more rain soon or simply the onset of night. The shadow from the stubborn child clung around her like a lover as she strode out of the villa and headed for the shore.

The thought of the heaped-up merlin lured her on. She knew he would still be there, and now she had worked out how to use him.

At the cliff's edge she couldn't look down in his direction at first. The sand ahead was grey with rain. Directly below, it was scuffed and scored. Morgan stared out to sea and wondered whether she really had seen a larger vessel the night before, or if it had been another of her conjurings.

She eased her way along the soaked tussocks to the head of the path. Glancing towards the nearer headland, her eye finally fell on the merlin. *Don't think* . . . She had to exert herself somehow. This way would be as good as any. She would bury him herself.

Swaddled by shadow, she descended with her head held back. With each step lower, the temperature seemed to rise. She had an idea that eyes were on her. Maybe it was the men who had lit the ridge-beacons; in the end they would have to come down. Maybe Mordred himself was watching from somewhere up by the villa.

She looked all around as she crossed the wet sand. The land reared above, meeting the new night with pale horizon fires. Bladderwrack cracked beneath her feet. She stooped to pick up a thread of seaweed and licked it against her thigh, just as little Anna had done. The ground down here felt alive; more pregnant than herself. Teeming with its own possibilities.

She crossed to the rock that had dashed the man's brains

out. Dove-grey, smooth, maybe from one of the graves. The earlier driving rain had not cleaned the streaks of blood; they looked like veins of red gold.

The smell from the flesh nearby was foul – too foul, it seemed, for all but the hardiest flies. Morgan was glad the rain had plastered his hair across his face. His leather jerkin and leggings, caked with gulls' mess, hid any other decay. *Don't think . . . Don't . . .*

She looked behind her. All the cairns in the man-garden had gone, which made the dead merlin in front of her look even more out of place. He was curled up tight, like a huge indissoluble rainspot crashed down from the skies. There was no show of blood. His skin, where she could see it, was eye-white. His hands appeared to be folded into his groin. *A seed sown in darkness . . .* She hated him. She loathed his whole race with their dogmas of wars and destinies.

'And what will it be this time?' she muttered down aloud, laying a soft hand on her stomach. '*Who* will it be this time? . . .'

She closed her eyes and wanted to say more. Not a funeral oration; more in self-defence, perhaps in belated revenge. *Liar*, she thought, but even that was wrong. Now she in turn was making it all too simple.

The black flesh cross arose in her mind. She had no case to make – nothing to set against the merlins' own version of what had happened before. And not just because she felt absurd here trying to hector a carcass.

She shook her head, but the darkness wouldn't fade. Arthur, Arthur . . . All she had ever wanted was not to be alone, not to be left behind when the warrior-king went to Guenever and peace replaced the war. Maybe she *had* played with fire at first, but she was the one who had then been burned. So terribly badly burned.

The heat around her increased. Her head filled with unusual words, at least one of which was a name she knew: *Moronoe . . . Mazoe . . . Gliten . . .* They seemed to be peeling off the sea at her. *Glitonea . . . Cliton . . . Tyronoe . . . Thitis . . .*

She stared forlornly at the merlin. He looked so small on that vast shore, and the shore itself was dwarfed by the sea. Both man and sand looked like reparations to the waves. This was all so much larger than herself. *Who will it be this time? . . .* She dropped to her knees and began to scoop a pit.

The sand came in sodden fistfuls. Soon she turned and sprayed it back behind her like a dog. Twice she rose to stumble away, to breathe in smokier air and flex her stiffening knees. On each return the flies dispersed to leave her to her work. As she did so, the darkness and noise in her mind dissolved.

She didn't plan to bury him deep, just get him out of sight. When her hollow was about a third as high as herself, she stopped. She stalked around the body, still gibing, 'Who? Who? Who this time? . . .' Then, facing the sea, with one push from her heel she rolled him in.

As he fell, his head seemed to unhinge. Its innards leered up, red and springy hard. Morgan looked away aghast. The flap of flesh was not his tongue. The women must have done it, before they left. Mordred had killed him, but the seven must have slashed at him and fed him on his own penis.

When she looked again it was worse. The prone corpse still moved, but now of its own accord.

There, in the pit, its arm had risen to its hidden face, and the fingers of its hand were picking at the stitches. Tugging, ripping. Morgan heard the cheek-flesh shred like linen. She couldn't breathe, couldn't move, just turned one shoulder towards it as if it might rear at her.

Illusion, illusion, she screamed at herself. Like the cuts and the night-fright; her mind running wild. But the mirage persisted.

The hand worked on fast, releasing the mouth, and out came the first buried testicle. The creature spat and gagged. Morgan stood as if staked. It grunted beneath her, hissed, trying to use its mouth, trying to make words come. The hand fell limp, the neck came up a little way, but still the freed face was obscured by its hair. For me, Morgan thought, left for me to deal with . . .

'You will know him when he comes,' came the dried-out, torn-mouthed answer to her gibes from before. Each word word clawed separately at Morgan. 'You will know him from his mark. He will be king. Once and future, lord of all . . .'

Morgan staggered backwards, turned, and in her delirium she started to run. As she did so, her waters broke.

Half-way up the path, she paused for breath.

The merlin lay face down in his shallow open grave. Or was he now some way beyond it? Closer to where the cairns no longer stood, and where she now sensed further disturbance? Morgan couldn't afford to care. This place defied all understanding. Glancing back farther, she saw a barge.

Empty, it seemed to have burst up through the water. Only moments before, there had been nothing between the tide-line and horizon. Then she saw the saturated figures behind it, pushing until it ran aground. They were back – the women – as if they had known they would be needed.

But 'back' was not the word. This was a new shipment. Much younger than before, barely adolescent. Sandy-haired and leggy, squealing with their effort. Just one, the eighth, was older. Tall, shapely, her hair tied back in a sodden cloth. She waded in apart from the rest, maybe giving orders, as lovely as young Guenever. But there was no Anna.

Morgan turned and climbed higher towards the smoke. *Moronoe . . . Mazoe . . . Gliten . . . Glitonea . . .* She wasn't going to stay on that gruesome shore a moment longer. She wouldn't have the child down there. If these were to be her midwives, then she would show them where they must come.

Their voices shrilled on the darkening air. Urgent cries now, but not addressed to Morgan. She didn't break step. *Cliton . . . Tyronoe . . . Thitis . . .*

A scream – brief and strangled – flew up from the shallows. A second shortly followed. Morgan kept walking; she was having her baby. She could think of nothing else, not even the corpse that had talked.

'Stop! No! Don't! . . . *No!* . . .'

This came from closer. A single voice flooding the babble, deep and plainly terrified. Morgan paused, clutched at her armlet and looked back.

At first in the dimness the sight made no sense. It looked like some composite creature careering towards her. Either that, or the well-made young woman had sprouted new limbs.

But a man was behind her, gripping her middle. Mordred. Tight up behind, hustling her on with each stiff-legged stride. Past the ghoul-merlin, without a glance down. The woman seemed to be trying to fold herself in half. Her feet weren't touching the sand, her head was bowed as low as her waist. Between her cries and gasps she was trying to bite herself free.

'See now! See!'

This time the voice was Mordred's. He was yelling up at Morgan, his eyes like eggs about to burst all over the girl. She wasn't much more than a girl, but she looked even more statuesque now in her soaked blue scrap of a dress. The kind of woman that Morgan might have expected Mordred to like.

'What? . . .' she bawled at Mordred over the din. 'See what? I don't care. The baby's started . . .'

'*Look!*' he ranted, thrusting the girl on to the cliff-path. '*Now* don't you see?' He held her with just one sinewy arm, as with his free hand he jabbed a finger at her. There was a completely new edge to his dementia.

His captive thrashed madly in front of him. Her long red hair broke out of its binding and flailed across her face. Morgan's hand fluttered up to grip her own throat. She was glad she couldn't see the face. Not another face.

'Please . . .' she began, making to turn and climb higher. 'No . . .'

'Tell me what you see!' Mordred snarled again. Morgan was stopped dead by the sight of him grabbing her hair and wrenching back her head, as if she were a horse whose teeth he wanted seen.

She saw the mark before she saw the face. The mark told her everything.

The young woman was gagging. He had bent her so far back that Morgan was afraid for her spine. The hand that had been round her waist, she noticed, now clutched one of her splendid breasts. 'Come on,' he roared up. 'Say!'

Morgan could only stare, holding her throat with one hand, her belly with the other. She couldn't even tell him to free her. It's her mother, she shouted inside herself. It must be her mother. But the mark said it wasn't.

'I knew her name!' Mordred rasped. 'I knew *her*. Not as a child, but like this.' He jerked her head back even further, pressed her breast harder. 'I knew her. I *had* her! She was my brother's *wife*! . . . Look!' He wrenched up the bloated breast. 'She's just had his damned child! . . .'

Moronoe . . . Mazoe . . . Gliten . . . Glitonea . . . Morgan saw the wet girls huddled like silent sea-nymphs by the barge. They could have been anyone. Please

121

God, anyone. They didn't have to be the same seven from before.

The woman twisted from side to side as she jabbed her elbows into Mordred, kicked her bare heels into his shins. She looked as if she were bursting from inside him, trying to thrash and clamber out. The mark at her hairline was undeniably the same; larger, fainter, but the same. Her hair too: longer, cleaner, but just the same colour. The wide eyes, pretty nose . . .

'It's the sea,' Mordred howled at Morgan, flinging his free arm at the girls. 'They've all grown backwards in it. It takes them in and twists them up in time. But not me and you, not me and you . . .'

At last he dashed the frantic woman to the ground. In the same movement she scuffed herself to her feet and skittered up the path like a spider missing half its legs. Morgan laughed with shock as she flew by.

She was over twenty years of age; certainly no younger. Three days earlier she had been eight. Just the night before, she had raised her arms to be carried through the water to the barge. Now the barge was back and so was she: Anna.

Cliton . . . Tyronoe . . . Thitis . . . Morgan closed her eyes and the sea-birds sneered louder. Did they too flock back and forth in time?

Don't think . . . The roll-call came again. *Moronoe . . . Mazoe . . . Gliten . . . Glitonea . . .* The water's laws were all its own. Morgan had imagined the women out fishing at nights, maybe trawling the waters for corpses. But they hadn't been scouring the sea for men at all. They had just left the land to turn into themselves. Their older, younger, sea-changed selves.

'Not me and you . . .' Mordred growled again in a wretched kind of triumph. Morgan opened her eyes to find him closing on her. By instinct she backed away, gripping her armlet. It was too much, all too much.

'Oh, you can't go anywhere.' he growled, his knife bouncing on his thigh. 'There's nowhere else to go to.' He jerked his head at the ridge. 'It ends there. Don't you see what's happening? This is all that's left. Except for what we've brought with us.' He waved a furious hand at her belly. 'Except for that now. Except for what we've brought *back* between us . . .'

Morgan threw her hands over her ears. 'Stop, stop! All I know is that the baby's coming, and that I am its mother and you are its father.'

'Father!' he cackled. 'You just don't see, do you?'

He was losing himself fast. Although he stood still, the air seemed to be skidding off his surfaces. Currents that Morgan couldn't feel on herself were buffeting him, twitching his hair, making him narrow his eyes as if through a sudden new squall of rain. It frightened her. She needed him now.

She tossed her head in the women's direction. 'Easy now,' she said to Mordred, shaking off her own torment only because his was so much more obvious. 'Whatever's happening . . . it's just them. The women. It doesn't have to touch us.'

He glared at her. 'But don't you see?' he pleaded, and for a moment she thought he might seize her. 'It hasn't touched us. Time. The sea. We came here as we were. Dry. Just as we were when we left the other place. And I know who you are! So what does that make *me?* What does it make us?'

Morgan searched his face, confused. In response he just shivered at her, and then with a shout hurled himself up the track after Anna.

'Don't leave me,' Morgan called, but too softly for him to hear. Briefly she stood rooted, poised between the transformative tide below and the land above that was transfixed in time.

The darkness quickly thickened, that of the night and the child's seeping shadow. *Cliton . . . Tyronoe . . . Thitis . . .* Morgan knew the seven untried girls were still in their huddle. Not her midwives, after all. They needed Anna with them, but Anna wasn't there. *I had her . . . My brother's damned wife . . .*

And when he caught up with her he would try to have her again, if only to put himself further away from Morgan. But Anna wasn't for him. No more than Guenever had really been for Arthur. Morgan touched her stomach. *What does that make us? . . .* Already she had an inkling, and she couldn't afford to care. Don't think, don't think . . . Only the baby mattered. Only that.

With new resolve she followed them up the path. The baby was so busy now. She walked as if she were stepping over it with each stiff swing of her legs. The smoke from

124

above had obscured half the villa. But when she looked beyond it, she saw lights. Nearer than the beacons. Torch flames coming down fast from the ridge. As many torches as there were stars. All the constellations made blood-red and swarming.

On she went, hurdling her own unborn child, both hands on her belly. Mordred, she mouthed as she came to the outbuildings. Mordred, my Mordred. He had come here for her, just to be with her . . .

The night felt tired against her but drew her on regardless. The birds had followed from the shore, their wails seeming to deepen the darkness. The sky and earth were sliding closer. A gull carped directly above. An answering noise flew up, like a copy of the bird's cry. It rose from the joinery.

The door was ajar. Morgan could almost smell him on the clouded air. Mordred, in there. But that hadn't been his cry. He could no more have made it than he could have given birth to their child. The cry had been a woman's.

It came again, shriller, fuller. The night's hands still brought Morgan on. When she rested against the doorway, the woman gasped in the fatter dark. 'Come . . .' she seemed to be saying.

Morgan let a spasm pass as she searched for a shape inside the hut. For a crazy moment she thought Guenever was there. Awaiting the newborn now, just like before.

'Tell me,' Mordred's voice then rasped, but not to Morgan – from over in the corner where she had failed to make him hers. 'Say how . . . Say why . . .

Tell me what comes next. Tell me what the child will be *for* . . .'

They were together on the ground. Morgan heard their sounds. Briefly she wanted to be them, become them, like the women of the sea who kept turning into themselves. But there was nowhere in their shadow for her.

She stepped into their steepling sound. Outside she heard murmurs and the crack of flames. Men's murmurs. The men from the ridge. Closing, closing, because of what was happening here. The world was shrinking where Morgan stood. She was drawing the whole of it to her, sucking it up inside.

The hands of the night were on her again, tighter now, at her waist, her hips. She seemed to be soaked from head to foot, as if her waters were breaking in from beyond the hut. Tidal waters, sweeping her forward from the men who were closing.

'Be with me now,' she called to Mordred, her voice all calm authority. 'Be with me here while I have this baby.'

She stooped to reach out. *Playing* . . . Her hand gripped a shoulder. Bare, lean, streaked with a mass of soaked hair. Morgan was half-supporting herself, half-trying to prise this higher body away from the lower. They could have been two halves of the same creature. She could have been trying to sever a centaur, but sever it she would. No one could stop her.

Her hand slid to the slim neck. A woman's. Not Guenever but Anna. Outside, men were all around.

126

Torchlight splintered through the cracks in the wattle. It looked like a hundred cuts, about to flow with red–gold blood.

Morgan smiled and sank to the ground. The bodies rose beside her. Slowly they separated. She saw him coming out of her, still large and curved, like a knife from its slot in a rock. And dark; almost black in the shadows. The new, altered Anna clung fast to his side. To Morgan's upturned eyes she looked like a shield at his shoulder; a riot of red hair, her long legs dripping down.

Mordred had one hand around her waist. With the other he cupped his sexual parts, as if he were about to hurl them in Morgan's face. The darkness was blood. There were other cuts on him too, all over, vanishing as she looked.

She held up both arms, still smiling. 'Be with me . . .'

Mordred drew Anna closer; her leg climbed his thigh, but above it she was straining away. He turned his head and Morgan's eyes met his. Her gaze served to break him down.

'. . . Not you and me,' came his voice, as if no time had passed since he had said the same words out on the cliff-path. To Morgan beneath him it seemed that the pumped-up flesh in his hand had spoken. Slow, emphatic, strangled. 'The water didn't touch you and me. We reached this place exactly as we left the last, at our own different times. And nothing changes here . . .'

'I know. I believe you, I know.' Morgan winced at

her first great tremor. She knew. She'd guessed. It passed all understanding, but she knew. 'Time has stopped here, yes, I know . . .'

Mordred raised a hand to silence her. Anna slipped towards the door, scooping up her dress as she passed. *What does that make me?* Morgan held his gaze, aware that he was about to tell her. But she knew. She wanted to laugh. *A second chance* . . . she remembered almost fondly. He dropped to his haunches and she saw his face convulsing.

'You're Arthur's sister. You had his child,' he grinned with his lips inturned; still he was big between the legs. 'And I am his son. The son you had before coming here.' His voice dropped to the faintest low scrape: 'They've twisted up time to make us mate. You and me. We wanted it. And you're my mother.'

Morgan felt the baby surge inside. Diving towards new darkness. She knew she would sink no deeper now. The waters around her were calming themselves. Peace, Christ might just have cried, be still . . .

Mordred had backed away. His glazed eyes were fixed on her belly; he seemed to be seeing through her skin to where the child thrashed inside. Morgan stared across at him, breathing faster now, but he didn't see. He had no eyes for her. All he saw was the struggle. And Morgan needed no more from him, now, than that. She just required him to watch. Her son, her son . . . *Don't think* . . . She had no idea if Anna was still with them. Beyond her vision the men from outside were quietly entering. The Great Remaking: a king to be made for a kingdom.

'You killed your father?' Morgan breathed at Mordred.

'I did what they wanted.' His voice was tiny, as if it had been relayed from that other awful world. His eyes widened on the word 'they'. Morgan understood. The men seeping in like smoke now. Land Men. The merlins from the ridge above. 'He came into me as he came into you. I took him on.'

You will know him when he comes. You will know him from his mark . . . It fell into place. She saw it all and started to smile at the pure grisly perfection of it. 'But he didn't die?' she gasped and felt weightless.

'Didn't die, no. I brought what mattered into this place, what makes him who he is.' He brandished his sexual organs at her. 'Brought him in here. His mind in my blood. I've been used. You've been used. They've played with us to make him all over again: the king, the king . . .'

Morgan, floating, closed her eyes. 'He's coming now,' she gasped, resting back on her elbows in the straw and raising both knees. It was all she could do. 'He's coming back . . .'

He had never really been away. The Once and Future King. And even though she felt no pain, she screamed.

It was nothing like before. None of the first time's tearing and clawing. Morgan felt as if she barely had to be there.

Mordred, now dressed, watched his mother's new

labour from a corner like a bad child banished. Constantly he fingered his knife, his face twisted into an unreadable rictus. He didn't look like himself. More like his own harrowed soul, showing itself only now as he, too, was turned inside out.

The merlins closed without a word. Arthur's Men, as ever. Morgan's contractions drew them in, setting a rhythm for the whole of the island. She was vast. She could have sucked up seven kingdoms into the space she would soon be making.

It wasn't like before. But again she disowned what would come. The child would arrive on a sea all its own. She closed her eyes when the spasms ran together. She saw the baby as a barge. She was the wind that had first filled its sails, but that didn't mean the barge was hers. Soon it would be powering itself, leaving her behind.

The merlins waited in a ring. Morgan smiled from face to face. Some smiled back, but not in encouragement or even sympathy. Like Mordred their eyes went inside. All that mattered was the child. The new son that wouldn't be hers; the son that had once been her lover.

Her bowels opened, but the merlins didn't recoil. Nothing she did could affect them. Already the stench in there was rank. So much rancid animal dirt. *Bull, bear, goat, ram* . . . Two of the merlins had knelt at her feet. Unwrapping her undergarments, they blocked her view of Mordred. She was glad she couldn't see him. See her first son. See his knife.

The merlins' hands were soft against her. They might

have been genuine midwives. Gentler, in their way, than Guenever had been. She twitched at one sharper touch, almost like the edge of a blade. Just a finger-nail, though. They were smearing her cleaner with spit, hair and hands. All for the child now, all for the child. She happened to be outside it. It could have been worming its way from a wood-block, not a womb.

The darkness quickly deepened. The night wound tightly round her: all the nights since she'd been here. Black on black on black. She thought she heard a different song. The softest choral murmurs. Rising from the shore, no doubt. Past the girls and through the bodies. Still she felt no pain.

The baby had kept all the hurt to itself. She was being born into it. They all were. Already its shadow encircled them. A roof beneath this roof. A sky within the sky. A harsher darkness lining the night. Morgan threw back her head and pointed her pelvis.

The merlins sighed in ecstatic recognition. They had seen the head.

He came up like a sword through water.

Morgan wouldn't look, but pictured him greeting the merlins – hand gripping wrist, even before he had been fully unsheathed.

She ground her teeth, knowing that she would never fully be delivered. Like her brother after he first entered her, this child would never leave. She would carry both for ever. And both were the same. She knew before she saw. A second chance, a second coming . . . This child was the beast-king reborn; with Mordred she had made the dead rise incorruptible; the child had been father to the child.

It was out of her, squalling. The afterbirth slid down. The song was louder now, a wordless hum that made the hut vibrate. The merlins were making it. The air and the smoke were playing it out of them.

Morgan craned her neck. The creature was on her, its cord still uncut. She saw the mark before she saw the face. Puffy, dark, high on the shoulder. No random birth-mark. The same as before; the same dark welted cross. She put up her hands and pushed the bloodied thing away.

'Take it,' she laughed. 'It's not my son . . .'

But the child came back into her hands. 'Hold it. *Have* it!' barked a voice that belonged to no merlin.

Morgan looked.

Through the blur of her tears and tiredness she saw Mordred crouched over her, coolly animated now. For the first time he looked fully awake – as if he too had just been reborn, this time with all his wits about him. With one hand he was pressing the jellied, puling mess up into Morgan's breasts. In the other he held his knife.

'Keep him!' he cried. 'You can't give him up. They had him the last time, and see how it ended! They made him how he was, made him fit their stories. It's for us to choose now. For us to decide!'

Two of the merlins were pawing him from behind.

trying to reach for the baby. 'No . . . !' Morgan howled as she saw Mordred jab back his arm.

He whirled around and stabbed the other twice in the neck before finishing off the first.

'No . . . No . . .'

Morgan held the baby close as if to shield its gore-caked eyes. Neither merlin made a sound as he died. Nor did the third, fourth or fifth try to avoid the insatiable blade. It seemed to be leading Mordred's arm, hurling him around the hut. If Morgan had doubted that here was Arthur's son, the proof was now running in rivers. But where the father's feats had stirred her, the son's had no effect.

The light through the chinks had faded. The baby's gums were rooting near her nipple. Her protests grew inaudible. But the din of the song seemed to rise with each killing. As if the man possessed by the knife were stripping away the clamour's husk to hear it in its fullness.

Logres, Logres, Logres, Logres . . . Hosts now intoning it. Amphitheatres alive with it. The sound was breaking up through the ground. Hell's music booming through its opened gates. *Logres, Logres, Logres* . . . Swooping and circling – hailing the baby: the new king born in a stable.

Morgan found the strength inside to scream above the cries.

Mordred came back to her. His mouth was wide open, his tongue lolled out. He stood above her, one bloody foot planted by either thigh. The baby had slid from her stomach to the straw. He stooped, blank-eyed, and took it up.

As he lifted the knife again, Morgan felt nothing. Nothing as the sound died around them but lived on in the dark. With a single upward thrust he slashed at the cord. Then he knelt in his spread of dead male midwives, took the knife between his teeth, and competently made the knot. He cut off the cord that was left and thrust it inside his tunic.

'It's not your son,' Morgan sobbed at him. The whole of her body seemed poised to fall apart. They were dwarfed by the newborn. Pygmies in its shadow. *The beast that was, and is not, and yet is.* 'You know it's not your son. He's come back through us, that's all. How can you think there's a choice for us now?'

Mordred glanced behind him. His mouth was still open, as if he couldn't yet take in the stench of so much life and death. Morgan saw only the mark. The baby's cries gathered strength. 'You should feed him,' he said in the flattest of tones.

Morgan glared back, defiant. But her eyes weren't enough. This fully woken Mordred was more of a match for her than before. He glanced behind him again. Maybe he gave a curt nod. It could only have been to Anna. Then he turned and picked his way over the tangle of slaughtered merlins, taking the reborn Arthur out into the night.

Morgan sank back into her pool of faeces and afterbirth. *Everything you need . . .* Mordred might have surfaced at last; but she now, in turn, was sinking back inside herself. The carnage around her stank like a ritual sacrifice, a hecatomb to the newborn. Arthur. Oh Arthur, still.

He had come again in blood. So he would go on. So he always had.

Part Three

FIRE

NINE

Mordred slipped the filthy baby inside his tunic and followed Anna out.

He was still so shaken, he could hardly walk. But he knew that he had been right to decimate the merlins, if only to slow down this process, to give himself some breathing-space. The tiny king-elect might not be his son, but that didn't make him theirs. Not yet. Not until he knew what came next.

The merlins outside the joinery didn't try to block his path. This dozen, like the five inside, looked incapable of landing a blow between them. Some looked deader already than the one he had killed on the shore.

The baby's noise was louder outside. As Mordred held it tighter, it felt like a hot coal on his chest. That, at least, was welcome. From his first day in this sunny, scentless land he had felt numbingly cold.

Anna seemed to be floating ahead of him. In every

physical detail she was the woman he had loved before: his sister-in-law and surrogate mother. But whoever she once had been, she now was someone new and he had to keep in with her. For that reason if no other, he had to take her on her own terms.

Inside the high wall she led him down the colonnade. He knew where they were heading. As she drifted into the pool room he smiled, unsurprised. Like Anna herself, this villa had also existed in the old kingdom. Not beside the sea there, and in a far worse state of repair. But Mordred knew every corner of it from before. Knew it as Guenever's palace. The ruin where she had lived apart from Arthur in the kingdom's last grim days, and where Mordred had finally learned that the king was his own true father.

Back then, he had found the queen sitting in state by the indoor water. He readied himself now to find her again. But the pool room was dark and deserted. Two braziers burned coldly, and from them Anna lit the lamps.

The baby's stifled cries racked Mordred, but Anna seemed oblivious. Finally she went to a couch in one of the alcoves. Facing him she sat straight-backed, just where the queen had sat when he had approached her. Then she unfastened her dress at both shoulders.

Mordred crossed to her, lifted out the child and passed it down. Moments later it had found her breast.

He stepped back to the arch, where he sank to the floor and tucked his knees up to his chin. Anna didn't raise her eyes. He couldn't begin to guess what role

140

she was playing in all this, though he now regretted his senseless, interrupted attempt to force the truth out of her before.

He tried not to look too hard at the feeding child. Arthur: a king reborn – so different from the last time he had seen him.

He closed his eyes and saw again that maddened brute curled up in a cave beneath its own court. *It*, not *him*. Not so much a king by the end as a living condition of the peace he had once imposed. Barely living, though. Waiting for his son to come and roll the kingdom from his shoulder.

But Mordred hadn't killed him; he'd known it even then. Locked in that cave's darkness, so much more had happened between them. The old Arthur had needed to die, so Mordred had taken his life – dutifully, almost literally. He had taken the life from that sorry blood-crazed hulk so that it could be lived again in some better place, in some better way. He had carried Arthur's mark out of that falling world so that the king could come again. And now, by this sickest of miracles, here he was.

He took out the sliver of cord and twisted it around his fingers. Playing with it steadied his nerve. Absently he passed it between his teeth to suck off the jellied mess. He knew he was tasting his mother's insides, but that didn't stop him. When the child had come free, he had stared between the merlins into Morgan's new dark emptiness with such longing. Then he had seen the mark high on the baby's shoulder. He saw the mark before he saw the face. Now he saw it again, royal purple on pink, as Anna eased the infant Arthur from one breast to the other.

'The Land Men were meant to have him,' she finally said, still not looking up.

'Land Men?' Mordred's voice was quaking, indistinct.

'What you call merlins, strays.' As if she hadn't once used the same terms herself, and always in this same disparaging way.

'And then what? What would they have done with him?'

As the baby sucked she wiped off its blood and gore with the hem of her dress. Then she glanced up. 'It's not for me to say. We women only start things; it's for the Land Men to carry them on to their end.' She paused. 'Maybe you should have asked them.'

Already Mordred had unsheathed his knife. Carefully he wound the cord around its hilt, then clamped it on tightly with his right hand. She couldn't make him feel guilty about the killings. He knew from before that for every merlin's mouth he silenced, two more would grow in its place. There was no beating them. Their words were in the air before they lived and stayed there for ever after they died. He might as well have tried to still the wind by ripping a pair of sails apart.

'Why should you want to keep the child?' she asked as if mildly amused, stroking its long jet hair. 'Do you feel like its father?'

Mordred stretched the cord taut between both his hands and said nothing.

'He is the king,' she told him unnecessarily. 'He has come to rule Logres.'

He'd heard that name before, when the women brought him on their barge. 'Is that what you call this place?'

'No. Here we're in Avalon.'

Mordred's eyes narrowed. She made it sound like a condition, not a country. The merlin on the shore had said the same. But Mordred had sensed from the start that he hadn't really left the kingdom behind. To him this felt like no new world, just a fragment of the old. The last of ancient Albion, salvaged from the deluge unleashed by Arthur's fall. An Ark of land afloat in a sea of twisted time.

Avalon. It stretched, the merlin had said, as far as the eye could see. Which was true enough, but no farther than that. The ridge which ran from headland to headland was its limit. Again and again Mordred's attempts to walk into the mists beyond had brought him back to his starting point. This ledge of land was all there was. And it had to be the timeless essence of old Albion; just as he himself had carried the living essence of Arthur.

'The merlins, then, would ship the child away to Logres?' he asked.

Instead of answering, Anna put a finger to her teat and drowsily the baby's head lolled. Mordred stood at once, putting away his knife. 'He's had enough,' he said. 'I'll take him now.'

Anna supported the child's neck while pulling up her dress with the other hand. 'Take him where?' she asked.

He looked into her eyes, amazed that he had been able to hold even this much of a conversation, and so soon.

'Why are you here?' he asked. 'You and the other seven?'

'To do what we can. To make the land ready. To make sure that it all begins.'

'Begins again, don't you mean? Don't you just want it all to be the way it was before, now that you've got the king back to rule?'

She passed up the child, then folded her hands in her lap. 'No. It doesn't have to be the same. This would be a new beginning, a second chance.'

'A second chance for the king?'

'For everyone.'

'Including me?'

She looked at him differently then, as if she had just seen through him. 'You're afraid for yourself? Why should you fear for yourself?'

Mordred's fingers reached for the mark on the baby's back. The feel of it took him back, although he wasn't quite sure to where.

'Your mother,' Anna went on quietly, 'appeared to be happy enough to hand over the child.'

His mother. Mordred nodded. 'She's not my mother. Not here.'

Anna's eyes widened, then she too nodded. 'As you say. And you want to be with her here? To stay with her now?'

'What does it matter to you what I want!'

His sudden anger had no impact. 'It matters. But you

can't keep the child and have Morgan too. She wouldn't agree to that. It's one or the other.'

Mordred glared at her – as remote and impassive as Guenever herself when first he had stumbled into her presence. The child had grown heavy against him. Carefully he put the sleeping creature back inside his tunic, and without another word to Anna he left the room.

Passing down the colonnade, he half-expected to see Morgan by the fountain. But she wasn't there. If she didn't follow him down from the joinery soon, he would have to go to her. But he was glad she hadn't appeared. Glad not to be battered by her beauty for a while, by her legs and eyes and line. Especially her eyes. *Don't let her look at you . . .* the first merlin had warned even as he fell bleeding to the sand. *Don't look in her eyes . . .*

He wandered from room to room. Each rang with a silent echo – and not just from the past. So much was at stake here. Too much for him to calculate.

Dawn broke, and back in the colonnade Mordred saw beacon-smoke with its swirling flecks of ash. But he smelled none of it. He never had. All he could ever smell for sure in this Avalon was bodies. Human juices. The stink of Morgan's sexual heat. Even now he was catching it. Wafting up, pungent, on a strong breeze from the shore.

He stepped back through the villa and out onto the forecourt. A cordon of torches had been staked along the cliff's edge to either side of the path head. In spite of all, he had to walk towards it. Towards her. He couldn't resist. The odour clogged his nostrils as he approached. It had never been this powerful before – even when Morgan had straddled him in the joinery.

Close to the edge, he glanced down through the curling smoke. The tide was in and the narrow strip of sand immediately below looked blacker than the water. Mordred blinked, badly disconcerted.

He had never seen so many merlins. Like an army of invasion awaiting the order to embark. But there were no boats. And as far as he could see, no Morgan either. But the high fishy stink continued to gust up at him. This whole part of the land seemed to be in heat.

Intoxicated, he remembered the Round Tables. Explosive assemblies where a single merlin would spellbind great audiences with tales of Arthur's wars and matings. This was like the largest Round Table of all – with so many merlins that none of them needed to speak. Just by being there they threaded the sex-smeared air, spinning silent sermons round the smoke.

Very few of them were moving. Corpses lay among those who sat or knelt. Mordred thought he recognized several from the joinery; the seeping blood of one or two made dark haloes on the sand. He wondered why they had been carried so far down only to be left unburied. Others, darkly smeared and twitching, looked as if they had burst up from their graves.

He hugged the baby closer. The great black cloud's silence as much as its size was affecting him. But he couldn't go down, couldn't even think of speaking with them. Not yet. He just stood watching until the child woke up in his tunic. It made no sound, but as soon as it stirred, twenty or so of the faces below turned and looked up for the first time.

Mordred dropped his gaze. Through the tunic's fabric he touched the royal symbol on the restless baby's back. *It's one or the other* . . . They needed this child but so too did he. Apart from anything else, it was all he had to bargain with. In killing the king before, he had done the merlins' bidding – and maybe rightly so. But was he always bound to put flesh on the bones of their stories? Couldn't he now have a life of his own? Anna had talked about a second chance, but Mordred had never had a first.

He backed away from the eyes and the torches. Day had fully broken. But smoke had curdled the sea mist into a bilious-looking smog that Mordred wasn't happy for the baby to be breathing. He hurried it back to the villa as its cries for food grew shriller.

He found Anna sleeping on his old couch in the pool room. The baby's noise alerted her. At their approach she blearily swung down her legs and freed her breast. She took the child without looking at Mordred, drew up her legs again, juggled him a little, and fed him lying down.

Mordred, stepping back, noticed that her eyes were closed. For a moment he hovered, in case she should fall asleep again and let the baby drop. As if to reassure him, she opened one eye and almost smiled.

He retired to the smaller couch around the pool's corner. He was exhausted himself, but he watched closely until the feeding was over. The child seemed so helpless when he let himself look at it. Trusting and ravenous. He didn't feel like its father, as Anna had suggested, but he could hardly be unmoved. *It's not your son*, Morgan had hissed. Which was right but also wrong.

Through him, this infant had come here. The merlin hadn't had to tell him how. Mordred had known it all in his sleep. The woman putting herself across him, the hand reaching down and pulling him up . . . He had loved it all. Every moment. Like never before. But in his sleep he had thought that his captor-lover was Guenever, not Morgan. Never his own mother. And where was she now? Why didn't she come, at least to find out what had happened?

The soft, hoarse roar outside began to mesmerize him. *Logres, Logres* . . . He'd heard it before, without knowing what it meant.

Anna stood and brought him the sleeping child – wrapped in a cloth she had searched out – before she rearranged her dress. Her face was expressionless.

'You didn't speak with the Land Men?' she asked.

Mordred stared, then shook his head. He could imagine himself walking back and forth to that cliff-top until the child became a man. 'How long can this go on?' he asked her dreamily over the baby's head.

She drew up her dress on both sides and pushed back the curtain of copper hair from her eyes. 'How long do you wish it to?'

'You want me to give him up?'

'You must do what you think is right. The choice is yours.'

He snorted feebly. 'Like the choice I had in coming here? In making my own mother pregnant?'

'You're tired,' she answered. 'Sleep for a while. I'll see to the baby if it wakes.'

She walked on towards the kitchens.

Mordred took out his knife and laid it on the floor beside him. There was room on the couch for the child as well as himself. He set it down on its side, then curled himself around it. The position felt good, natural. But deliberately, still, he didn't look hard at its features. He couldn't afford to be drawn. Even as close as this, he had to keep some distance.

Soon he was sleeping. Anna's footsteps ran rhythmically through his dreams.

Twice the child started to snuffle. Each time, Anna's hands came down to remove it before Mordred could properly wake. On its return he rested his fingers on it protectively, glad of its warmth, soothed by its stillness.

Then he dreamed that the child was fighting back. Grappling him with hands that couldn't have been its own. Spitting, clawing, screaming abuse.

Mordred started awake as if a dog had barked nearby.

The baby had gone.

TEN

Mordred tumbled from the couch, scooping up his knife. Evening had closed in, but none of the lamps was burning.

'Anna!' he yelled. 'Morgan!' But the smell on the clotted air was the stink which had dizzied him at the cliff's edge earlier. The cemetery stench of that merlin shoal. And it seemed to be coming from the colonnade. So too did the menacing night-time chorus: *Logres, Logres* . . .

He closed his eyes and gripped the knife tighter. His nerve was deserting him again; he longed to topple backwards into the pool and end it all that way. But there was no way out for him; there never had been. Ever since surviving the slaughter at his own birth, one reprieve had followed another. He just kept on finding a larger darkness to suffer in. Like Arthur, he couldn't really die. Like the king, he would keep coming back for more.

The sound and smell drew him on through the arch, into the colonnade. He felt as if he was being led by his groin. His fingertips rubbed at the cord he had wrapped around his knife's hilt. He could sense the merlins' cordon all around – like a huge uncleaned umbilicus, closing in to squeeze the child out of the villa just as first it had been squeezed out of Morgan.

Breathing through his mouth, he entered the central courtyard. The deep male sound seemed to splash from the fountain, striking every stone to make a deafening echo. But there were no merlins. No Land Men. Only Anna, standing far away in the darkness, under the high stained statue.

The steepling water between them blurred her features and Mordred stepped aside to see her better. She didn't seem to have noticed him. Her hands clasped just below her chin, all her attention was on the fountain. She looked on the point of both recoiling and preparing to pounce.

Mordred followed her line of vision and from behind he saw Morgan, sitting curve-backed on the marble slab in an unfamiliar green gown. Her long black hair had been braided and coiled so that the white of her slim neck shone in the gloom. Mordred knew she had the baby. She hadn't just taken it down to the shore. Again he glanced at Anna, but failed to catch her eye.

The torrent of noise crested and fell away to a soft burr. The cries of the night birds broke through. They sounded unreal now, impossibly remote, as if they were singing from inside their own eggs.

Mordred took three steps sideways and Morgan heard his sandals on the mosaic. She turned her head to look at his legs as he came round. It was the first time he had seen her face painted – subtly, sparingly, bringing up the full wolfish beauty of her lips and high cheeks. Her gown was opened at the front, the baby's head against her breast.

Relieved though he was to see the child, Mordred shook – unsure if she were suckling or suffocating it. Then there was a flutter of movement. The infant's arms jerked as Morgan passed it from one tough-tipped, blue-veined breast to the other.

It fastened itself on and she looked up with a smile that Mordred found unfathomable. *It's in her eyes,* the first merlin had said. *She did it with her eyes . . . She was the king's bad side made flesh, the king's evil, she had to be his queen . . . she couldn't be left behind . . .*

Like Arthur before him, Mordred had no defence against those eyes. He wanted her, he wanted her. She could have been anyone; she happened to be his mother. All he had to work out now was how much that still mattered.

'Please go,' he said to Anna above the soft chaos, the sexual stink searing the back of his throat.

She too looked lovely. But her beauty, like Guenever's, crept up on you slowly. Morgan's at once took you captive. Mistrustfully Anna turned her eyes away from Morgan, then bowed her head and began to skirt the fountain crabwise. She slipped behind the closest smoke-smothered column and Mordred was alone with his mother.

He didn't know where to put himself, so he sank to the ground and sat cross-legged, setting the knife down beside him. Morgan was absorbed in her feeding; hiding behind her huge dark eyes, not using them to bait him. But her fierce musky scent was doing that already. And Mordred drank it in. Within moments he had forgotten almost everything but her.

He saw that she had painted her nails as well as her lips, that there was gold now at her neck and wrists. *She had to be his queen . . .* Mordred hadn't seen this cool, majestic side to her before. He remembered her racing to the cliff-top that morning. What if he hadn't called up to her then? What if she had fallen and died with her baby? But he had called, and she hadn't fallen. Now the baby gnawed on. And Mordred glimpsed a chance of having it all.

'You look wonderful like that,' he breathed. His voice was so low and faltering that when she looked his way he had to say it again.

'It's relief.' She turned her eyes away, flipping a hand at her free, engorged breast. 'It hurts not to do it. I'm doing it for myself, not him.'

Him. On her lips the word sounded odd. Stressing the baby's maleness. Mordred blinked. Did you feed me? he wanted to ask. Did you ever? But in his heart he knew that the first time, like the second, she would have screamed for the child to be taken before she had even looked at it.

The smoke blew in heavy gusts across the open area. Half-substance, half-sound, with the smell wrapped tight around both. Mordred didn't know why she had brought the baby out here to feed it, but the child was no longer his main concern. She looked so good. She knew it too, but she never seemed vain. It was as if she weren't quite sure whether she liked herself under all the glamour — or, if she did, on quite what grounds.

She adjusted her breast and Mordred saw the mark on the baby's shoulder. As Morgan saw it too, her free hand fluttered up to the ugly dragon armlet that he had never seen her without. He'd seen her touch it often, just like this. Some superstitious tic.

'How did you ever survive?' she drawled at him, her eyes still on the baby. 'How did Guenever manage that? How did she keep you hidden?'

'Guenever?' Mordred hadn't known that the queen was involved. And to make sure he survived? She, more than anyone, must have wanted him dead.

He shrugged, shook his head. This wasn't what he wanted to talk about. He blinked, and to his astonishment tears filled his eyes. He knew only the merlins' tale: about the men sent out to levy all the May-born babies and then pack them off to sea in a crewless boat; about his own reprieve not by the queen but by old Nabur, the man he had called father for eighteen years in that bleak northern hill camp.

His lips sheared back against his teeth. He couldn't say any of this to Morgan. Hardly even to himself. Already it felt like somebody else's story; as if it had happened only to his own poor motherless shadow.

The mournful song from the shore swelled again.

Mordred picked up his knife and eased towards her on his haunches. She let the child come off her breast. Again it was sleeping. Earlier Morgan had spread out the cloth on the slab beside her; now she turned to place the naked baby on it. Closer to, she looked so sublime that it dazed Mordred. She moved to refasten her dress.

'No,' he gasped, putting out a hand. 'Please, leave it.'

She let her hand fall, then closed her eyes. Her breasts still stood high and hard. My mother's breasts, thought Mordred, undeterred.

In front of him sat a woman; that was all. The birth seemed to have removed any last reason for him not to want her. This second child's coming had wiped out the fact that he had been her first. He chewed on his lip, passed his forefinger over the hunt mosaic, and sank himself in the taste of her. The moment grew gloriously bloated.

'This smoke,' he said, tossing his head as if to disperse it.

Morgan re-crossed her slender legs. A woman showing him her breasts. A woman who could have been anyone. 'It's his smoke,' she answered, gazing way above Mordred's head at the ridge beyond the villa.

His. The king's. Mordred turned slowly to the child on the slab. It looked so stark on its back. Sacrificial. Every time he saw it, he thought of himself all those years before, but for Morgan it had been only days. His fingers curled on the knife's hilt.

'You can't keep him,' he heard her say. *You.* Her tone was severe. She could have been reminding him that two and one don't make twenty-one.

Mordred bent his head, seeing again that mess of waiting flesh on the shore. 'But do you know what we'd be giving him up to?'

'What if I did? There's no other way.'

He looked at her through a blur of new tears. He needed her to want this child more, needed to know that she wasn't indifferent.

'You don't know,' he said, 'and yet you were ready to hand him over.'

Her eyes blazed steadily at him through the kohl. Mordred stiffened in anticipation. 'That's what I do,' she told him with a tight smile. 'It's all I know.'

And in that dizzy moment Mordred wanted her twice as much as ever before. All her lines were so clean, the flesh on her limbs so spare. And in this dead light its pale tawny sheen made her look almost too exquisite to be real.

'You have no feeling for him?' Mordred whispered 'He *came* from you.'

She said nothing. Mordred's eyes wouldn't stop watering. She looked incapable, now, of any kind of feeling a all. He felt so cold. The shore-song filled the courtyard *It's one or the other . . .*

Her legs were still crossed. He reached out and began to stroke her higher sandalled ankle. If she flinched he didn't notice. Soon he was sliding his fingers higher under the hem of her gown, marvelling at her calf smooth perfection, slipping down then to grasp her other ankle. Maybe only moments passed, but they fel like months. This . . . he thought, I want this . . .

'When did you know?' she asked. 'When did you know who I was to you?'

He looked no higher than her neck. 'The merlin told me.'

'And you said nothing to me.'

'I wasn't sure it was true. How could I be sure?'

'But you said nothing.' She sounded implacable. Methodically she gripped and ungripped the armlet, as if she were trying to appease the trinket itself, or hide Mordred's closeness from its one bulbous eye.

'I couldn't. It was too big, too much.'

'And when I came to you in the hut, you still didn't say.'

He bowed his head. What did she want from him here? 'I couldn't. I can't. It's not in me.' His hand slid as high as the back of her knee.

'No,' she said.

Mordred felt cheated but also relieved. Reprieved from himself. He pulled away his hand, but only as far as her painted toes.

'No,' she said again, dragging together the flaps of her gown so emphatically that two spots of milk spilled on to Mordred's forearm.

He let her go, put his arm to his lips and, using only the tip of his tongue, licked the liquid from the hair. He knew she was watching; he wanted her to see. But still he had no idea where he was with her.

Then without looking at her he stood, sheathed his knife, and stepped up to where the baby lay: the child that wasn't his father, wasn't his son.

'They want him for Logres,' he told Morgan, frowning at the infant's chubby wrists, its perfect little fingernails, 'for a kingdom called Logres.'

'Logres,' she echoed. Her voice seemed to come from the fountain, up from its depths, like an oracle that Mordred had studiously been trying not to consult. But he had to ask her everything now.

'What,' he went on, 'do you think would happen to us then? To you and me?'

He looked at her when she didn't reply. Her great dark eyes were fixed on the child, half-murderous but half-motherly too. Even when they were downcast, she shimmered with authority. *She had to be his queen . .* Mordred saw how Arthur must have been tempted past all taboo to have her.

He shook his head, then took a step closer. His chest came level with Morgan's head. He seemed to have entered the sound-storm's eye, a tiny silent pocket in the din. Clearly he heard the catches in her breath. Madly he wanted to shield the sleeping newborn's ears from what it might hear.

'I can tell you nothing,' she said. And then she startled him: 'I don't want to do the wrong thing again.' And Mordred didn't know if she meant with the baby or with him.

'Maybe you didn't do the wrong thing before,' he answered, heaving. He sensed then that inside herself she too might be afraid. Too scared even to think about what she really wanted. He had to know more, find out more – for both of them. But also he needed more breathing space, more time to try to work out what lay in the balance. *It's one or the other . . .* But all he could see from here was himself losing again, ending up this time with less than nothing.

He flicked the cloth over the child, sniffed and stepped back into the maelstrom.

'Please,' he said, 'stay here with him.' He left before she could answer.

Night had come down like sacking. In the darkness the path to the cliff-top seemed steeper than before. Even if Mordred had stopped walking, the incline would still have tipped him down towards that awful shore.

But before he passed through the villa's front gateway, he heard footsteps on the chippings behind.

'Wait!' cried a woman's voice. Her words scythed through the maudlin drone that made the air as heavy as water around him.

He slowed a little and Anna came alongside. They were almost at the line of torches, although dense swirling smoke now dimmed the flames.

'You don't have to go down,' she said, and at once Mordred knew that he did. 'You can ask me what you need to know.'

'But if I gave up the child, would it go to you?' he asked briskly, walking on.

She didn't reply at once. 'No. Not in the first instance.'

'Then I have to speak with them.' He nodded seaward.

'The child will be safe. Do you need to know more?'

At the head of the path he smiled at her wanly. 'Why don't you want me to go down?'

She met his eye. There had been a tension between her and Morgan, on the shore on that morning of their fight and after. Plainly, too, there was tension between her and the merlins. She said nothing; but her arched eyebrows told him that it was all futile, that no amount of talk now could make any difference, maybe even that he couldn't win either way.

He turned and stepped on to the path. It seemed to reach down farther than before. No single merlin was in sight. The noise they all made wasn't so much inhuman now as all too human. The sounds that men – and women – made when no other language was necessary.

The torches on their poles above seemed to shed no true light. He peered over his shoulder. Anna was standing like a sentry in the smoke. He took some more steps down; still he could see none of the merlins clearly. The darkened patch they covered on the shore seemed smaller than he remembered. He wished he had some kind of a rope round his waist, a link back to Morgan in the villa. But he had no lifeline, only the cord wrapped around his knife which now he pulled out of his belt.

The air's texture thickened; its cloying, soily-sweet taste made his whole face ache. His faith was weak, but this felt like stepping down into the head of God. All the merlins were murmurs inside His mind, the sound of Him thinking. A fusion of what had been and what was yet to come. And the word that embraced it all was *Logres* – its rhythm now making the island vibrate.

Again he stopped. This was what Anna hadn't wanted him to see. The living and the dead had made an indiscriminate heap. Some of the merlins were half-buried in the sand; others appeared to be eating it. Writhing, flexing, a pile like a single person. A sheen clung to the mass. A slickness in the dark and smoke giving off its own putrid glow. Many of them were mating – their airborne roars were the loudest.

Mordred caught his breath. So much twisted sexual wreckage, as if it had all just been dumped ashore from some unholy collision at sea.

Once, as a boy, he had seen a colony of ants pre-flight. Millions of the things, drunk on each other and what they were doing. Appalled, but also drawn, he had put in his hand and sifted the long mucous chains of them through his fingers. The winged queens, in particular, had attracted him. But there were no queens here, none that Mordred saw. Just men. Men on men. Men in men. Warm flesh impacting like eggs on the crispier corpses.

'Speak now!' he shouted into the turmoil. 'Speak to me!' His voice clubbed through their sighs and simpers, which seethed up at once to a higher pitch. 'What will happen if I give you the child?'

'He will rule Logres,' the sea seemed to laugh at him. 'He will make the tide turn again.' Mordred felt that he'd been splashed by sound. The words came like a breaking wave, hissing and lapping at him from the feet up. On impulse, he stepped back as it continued to travel up his legs.

He shut his eyes and waved the knife stupidly in front of him, picturing these fabulously foul men feeding on one another. He had known that hunger himself, both here and in the kingdom. Known it too well. They're together, he thought, and fleetingly that filled him with envy.

'What *are* you?' he breathed back. The taste in his mouth was gorgeously impure, as if he were eating a cut from a beast still not fully dead.

'We're with you,' came back the cryptic reply, liquid as before, but thicker now than water.

Mordred shuddered as it dampened him. He needed to be touched. Not necessarily by Morgan – any hand would do; just a touch to hold him down. He parted his lips to speak and felt as if he were kissing the mouth of hell. His words came out as less than a whisper. He felt that he was talking to the whole of this land's history; the soul that beat beneath it:

'Help me.'

'He's not your son.' It sounded like an apology.

'I know. I know.' This wasn't the issue. Of course it wasn't his son – or only in the sense that a sailor is the sea's. The child was theirs much more than it was his. They could have it, they could take it to their Logres. In giving them the child he would also be getting rid of them. But where would that leave him – without his bargaining counter?

'It's not him that you want,' they soothed. 'Without

him, you'll have everything you need. Without him, she's yours. In any way you choose. Here you can have her. You can be *inside* her . . .'

Mordred took another step back. He'd been disappointed too often: too many hopes raised up, then dashed. The pit he stood in already seemed bottomless. He doubted that he would ever rise from it. He remembered the chaplain at his hill camp warning of the beast that would one day rise from just such a place: the beast that was, and is not, and yet is . . .

But he wanted to believe them, needed to so badly. He twisted around to see if Anna was still at the cliff's edge. For a moment the smoke and clouded light formed a different outline: huge, female, regal, straddling them all. Mordred narrowed his eyes. The shape reached behind its knees and pulled itself apart until, sensually slowly, it dissolved. And then it wasn't Anna up there but Morgan – just as he had seen her on that dawn of her dream, only now she held the baby.

'Bring him,' purred against his back. The sand was speaking to him; the sand, the sea, the stars that wouldn't shine. The merlins had re-entered the elements' realm and Mordred couldn't argue with the air. The air had always been Arthur's anyway. And these had always been Arthur's Men.

He drove himself back up the path. He couldn't see Morgan; she must have stepped back. He cast one last glance over his shoulder. Anna was near the water now, though he hadn't seen her coming down. A skiff bobbed in the shallows. The merlins writhed in front of it: choosing, not being chosen; directing, not being directed. Their flesh-feast rippled like a small tributary sea. Men inside a mixing-bowl. They were welcome to their baby.

At the top of the cliff the torches had guttered. They had all been ablaze before he'd gone down. Already time was sliding by at a different pace. A new dawn felt imminent. *The child will be safe . . .* He didn't doubt that. Even if he threw it down to them now, no harm would ever come to it.

A sharper scent came from farther up. He tilted his head, and like a dog tried to catch it again; the rising savour from the shore had swallowed it whole. But then he saw her. Morgan. Moving back towards the villa. This wasn't what he'd expected. From behind he could make out no more than the shape of her dress. Her arms appeared to hang loose at her sides.

Looking about him, Mordred saw no sign of the child. 'Morgan!' he called thinly. His first instinct, even now, had been to yell 'Mother!'

She didn't look back. The merlins' groans might have swamped his cry. She kept walking, but her distance from him didn't increase. He watched her gown fill with the breeze, making her look so supple. *Without him, she's yours.* He had to believe it. He had to take that risk.

'Mother!' he gasped, just loud enough to hear how it sounded.

This time she paused and turned. Her slowly-parting lips looked close enough to kiss. He had been wrong about her arms. In one she was cradling the baby as i fed from her. A cross-breeze pressed her dress against her, showing Mordred the length of her legs. There really had been no choice at all for him.

'No,' he murmured, still unable to move from where the merlins were converging. 'Bring him back. I'll do it now. Let me take him . . .'

She touched a strand of hair away from her temple, turned and made again for the villa. Mordred didn't understand. She seemed to be rising at a much steeper gradient than that of the slope, walking away on a stairway of air, prowling up to paradise ahead of him.

Without him . . . But still she had him with her: Arthur. Still a part of her. And she was taking him in the wrong direction. Mordred ripped himself away from the cliff's edge and set off in pursuit. He hadn't put his knife back in his belt. He wasn't yet sure that the moment to use it had passed.

The merlins' moaning grew no softer as he left the shore behind. He was bringing the sound with him. No distinction could be made any more between this place, the people in it, and the spirit which moved both.

He broke into a trot but came no closer to Morgan. He had known this before. For years in the old kingdom he had dreamed of chasing a distant figure, hunched but regal. The figure had always kept clear of the range of Mordred's drawn knife but also served as a scout, leading Mordred into the place where he had to be, where in the end he could kill and set free.

Morgan passed out of sight between the villa's portals.

Moments later Mordred followed her through, gratefully stepping into silence.

She was waiting by the courtyard fountain, where she had placed the child on the slab again. It looked so small and pale after the colony on the shore. Slowly Morgan raised a hand to touch her armlet as she stared at the baby. The Once and Future King. It flexed its leg and started to mewl.

Morgan's smell filled Mordred again: painted all over the smoke. He felt swollen numb. He had to have her. He would fight her if he needed to. She couldn't stop him now.

He sheathed his knife, went to her, seized her above both elbows and lifted her off her feet. When she came down he fastened his mouth on to hers.

ELEVEN

The baby's cries spiralled beside them. Morgan's tongue flicked Mordred's teeth and – jammed against her – he almost came. His mind was alive with the merlins together, regenerating their own decay down there on the shore, and then he saw the vast spread legs of that smoke queen on the cliff.

Morgan drove her tongue deeper as Mordred shuddered, raising her thigh to anchor him. She was the one who sighed then, soft into the pit of their mouths. Mordred felt her fingers close on him through his loincloth.

Dawn broke above them as if their embrace had released the night. 'I don't want to do the wrong thing again,' she whispered down his throat. And before he could speak, she tore away the loincloth. Suddenly she seemed to be pressing him in half a dozen different places at once. Inside her grip he felt the shape of himself as she might have felt it.

He started to move. For the briefest, dizziest moment he felt that he was entering himself. But then she let him go and tilted back her head. In his arms she looked wild-eyed but drawn, as if she had recently fed the five thousand and not just this baby squalling on the slab.

Without him, she's yours. The promise coiled around them in the smoke, lifted on the breeze.

'I don't want to do the wrong thing,' she told him yet again. The words washed over him; she could have been saying anything. The world began and ended for him in the space between her moving lips.

'The baby will be safe,' he echoed. 'He's needed, but not here. *We're* here . . .'

He tried to pull her back on to him. But she was peering at his neck, his uncovered arms. Already she seemed to have forgotten the child, oblivious to its cries. She touched his throat, then looked at her hand. 'Sometimes I see cuts on you.'

'It's not my blood,' he tried to laugh, and her eyes flashed at him. He grabbed her, closing one hand over the armlet. Brusquely she shook him off. 'What is this thing?' he said, flipping at its circular spine.

She touched it, let her hand drop. A raucous new series of shrieks broke from the child. Mordred knew that the band had come from Arthur: from him to her.

'Take it off. Give it to me.'

Eyes averted, she started to twist it down her lovely upper arm. Round and round, as if it ran on a grooved thread. Over her elbow, past her wrist. It looked thin, insignificant, as it dangled from her fingers. But the marks where it had bitten into her arm were thick and red. Mordred took it and thrust it over his own broad wrist. It unnerved him a little; it didn't belong with them. It would go the same way as the baby.

Morgan held her arm. Mordred reached out and cupped her breast. 'Just be with me,' he said. 'Here. Together with me. You'll have everything you need.'

She smiled at the trinket on his wrist, then bent to kiss the riot of hair just above it. 'Everything . . .'

He wrenched up her head and they kissed with peculiar bitterness. Mordred had drawn blood from her lips the first time. Now he tasted his own as the points of her teeth scraped his tongue.

She twisted her shoulders, broke free and took three steps to the side. Away from the fountain, away from the baby's bedlam. She wrapped her arms around herself and fixed her gaze high, on the smoke's dark smudges on the pale morning sky.

Mordred understood. She was showing him that she wouldn't resist, wouldn't even look. Perhaps she never had. She seemed almost impatient now, rubbing at her arm as if the larger sacrifice had been the dragon. His doubts swam back. He couldn't help feeling that still he might end with nothing.

He crossed to the fountain, stepping over his unravelled loincloth. Morgan watched askance, then turned her back on him completely. On them both.

Surprisingly, the crying child's eyes were open. Mordred lifted it without looking into them. 'Soon . . .' he said, close to its little head. Then he picked up its swaddling cloth, wrapped it loosely, and pushed up the dragon armlet until it lodged on his forearm.

'You know this is right,' he called to Morgan, loudly, slowly, putting equal stress on each word – as if they were all as unconnected as she was to the child. But he knew he was talking only to himself.

As he passed out of the colonnade he glanced back. Morgan was kneeling by the fountain, her face buried in his loincloth. Her shoulders were moving – too fast, he thought, for her to be crying.

He put the child's face to his shoulder and headed for the merlins' precinct.

The new day's light grew thinner. It seemed to be rising from the still-invisible shore ahead, dispersing across some equally invisible ceiling just above Mordred's head.

He turned to look back before he could make himself look down. The villa seemed worlds away, steeped in a shoddy sunlight that fell far short of the shore. He had thought from the start that each day here had simply been painted over the night. Inside all the dazzle, the dark kept burning cold.

He gazed past the villa where Morgan now knelt waiting. Up to the ridge where the beacons still burned. Again in their smoke he picked out the shape of a vast squatting woman, reaching beneath her thighs to pull herself apart and pour out this fragment of sand, grass and stone for them all to fight in.

He rocked the hot child against him, slipping a finger into its mouth. Abruptly it fell silent, but Mordred knew this couldn't last. He turned to the shore and let his eyes fall.

He had known he would be surprised, but not like this. Dimmed by dawn mist, the sea's horizon looked quite as high as the headlands to either side. A vast, stilled wall of water seemed to sweep down to where the sand began.

He had heard how once a sea had sheared itself apart to let a people through. This had to be a similar trick. Any semblance of waves, tides or spray had gone. This great grey-green face was like a plate bolted on to the sand to make a massive bowl or basin.

The child jerked feebly against Mordred's shoulder, as if it wanted to be turned to see too. 'Soon . . .' said Mordred, sliding his finger in further while new whimpers came out around it. Mordred wasn't listening. His attention had switched to the strip of shore below. At first he thought he had seen nothing and no one down there. On stepping closer to the edge, the figures came into focus.

Seven of them, female and naked, sea-changed again since their return with Anna. Once so pale, now they were all as tawny-skinned as the sand that they were almost choreographically trawling. Each nubile young woman trailed a dark length of debris. It looked like seaweed, but Mordred swallowed hard when he realized it was all the merlins' cast-off skins.

One last step took him to the cliff's edge. Directly below he saw that the old burial ground was serving as a refuse pit for the seven's rakings. The sand they had cleared was smeared rust-red in some parts, simply black in others. The smell drifting up was of heated iron and burnt skin; not carnal now in any way familiar to him.

The seven began to furl the disturbed sand back over the great filled pit. It took them barely any time. To Mordred, they seemed not to be moving from one side of the pit to the other; rather they flickered from place to place, fading then resurfacing, like visual echoes from another dimension. Even at this pass, it was impossible to watch and not be entranced. Impossible too for Mordred to look at what lay further up the shore . . .

Compelled by the dance, he took his first steps down on to the cliff-path. The baby squirmed in his grip. 'Enough!' Mordred grunted, shocked by his own queasy anger.

He knew he was leaving behind more than just Morgan and the villa. He was stepping down into an older, deeper place – deeper in the way that suicide is deeper than death. He saw it as an enormous cauldron, warmed by the fires that always burned below, bodily stirred by the movement of the women. And from it, soon, the most almighty storm would break.

Slowly he went lower. The sea's unbreachable wall soared above his head. He felt afraid, but he left his knife in his belt. He couldn't fight this underside of the night.

He looked past the women to the silent water. Although it was so dark, shapes shimmered inside it. Fluid in the stasis, images from the kingdom he had left behind: a conical hill like the one where Arthur's court had perched; the outline of the chalk giant on the hill near his own camp; ruined villas, broken walls, shanties of wood in the fragments of an amphitheatre, all floating, melting, fusing.

The standing sea was mirroring Mordred's memory, showing what had already been engulfed. These soft shapes had once been hard. His own drowned world had once been tinder-dry. Now it was all re-forming. Coming down on to the sand, he was aware that he had reached the frontier between two eras. This Avalon was not so much a place as a time, and yet it was no time at all.

He pushed the child higher and kissed its tear-blurred eyes. Then he twisted it, blindly pulled down the wrap and kissed its cross-mark too. The dragon band seemed to bite into his wrist. The baby shuddered and began to wail again. Mordred looked away, back at the women, still not along the shore to where he would have to take the child in the end.

The women stood in a crescent where the cairns had once been. Since any light here appeared to be rising, their slim legs looked paler than the rest of their bodies. Each had a large, dark pubic area that merged with the shadows under their breasts. None was moved by the baby's din. Blankly they all looked upshore, to where the skiff seemed to be stacked against the great wall of water – and to the hunched male figure beside it.

Mordred couldn't ignore him any more. He turned . . .

He had always imagined that he would have to deal with a man. A Land Man, too. But still he shrank inside himself to find one. It would, in a way, have been easier to dump the desperate baby in front of the crescent and then slink away. But the women weren't waiting. Not for him. They never had been. The man up ahead was. Just one man, where once there had been so many. The last and first of the Men from the Land.

He set off towards him along the curved line of water. Crouched beyond the skiff, the man's black-clad back was likewise long and curved. He fitted this place in a way that the tawny women did not. Like witches, their duty had been to tend this pot. This figure had been cooked from it.

The baby's wild noise bounced back off the steepling sea. The air inside the cauldron grew thinner by the moment, as if the child's unshuttable mouth were sucking out its substance.

This wasn't a simple hunger cry. No mess of milk could have stopped these screams. Mordred wondered if Morgan could hear them at the villa, wondered if they rang out as far as the waiting kingdom of Logres.

His step slowed as he skirted the grounded skiff. The man was wearing the hooded cloak from the villa. Mordred had worn it himself. Only Anna could have brought it down. He still hadn't turned, and Mordred guessed that he would not. Nothing ever got easier. Mordred still had to make the running.

He saw an elbow twitch. The arms were tight to his sides, but his hands could have been moving in front of him. The head was tipped back a little way, a sweep of sooty shoulder-length hair swayed.

It was hard to see more. The fractured images from the sea now flitted like fish across the sand to the cliff. Mordred squinted as they swirled: chapel walls in dissolution, sinuously-curling stretches of road, and even finally the flattened-out faces – huge, leering – of men he had known in Arthur's former Age.

Arthur, Arthur. The grit to that old pearl and again, very soon, to the new. Mordred pressed the child's face hard against him. Too hard. He was wanting to hurt it, to share the pain he could never quite leave behind. *Without him, she's yours.* In a dark part of himself he knew that even if this had been his own true son, he would still have been bringing it, and Morgan would still have been letting him. A child wasn't for them, and they weren't for children. They couldn't go that far past themselves.

The images clustered thicker. Some seemed so solid that Mordred found himself stepping around and under them. Towers taller than he had ever seen, glistening high-arched bridges, metallic birds swooping in chilling silence, leaving streaming clouds behind them. Already here was a world of sorts. One he would never live in: each person in it sliding isolated into the next, marching slowly upward in an ever-sadder spiral.

The soft sights cleared as he closed on the dark man. He had him almost in profile now, but a hang of hair obscured his face. Mordred wanted to yell with the baby instead of trying to silence it. He needed his own release.

The man had a pile of stones in front of him: a cone-shaped cairn. The noise at Mordred's ear became a hoarse roar, impossibly loud from such tiny lungs. The man was playing with his cairn. He reached forward to extract, with one spidery finger and thumb, a darkened sliver from the stones' apex. Not seaweed but a thin strand of weathered skin, supple, pickled perhaps, cloudy white with a darker vein running through it.

Mordred stopped six paces short and touched his knife's hilt. The cord was still wrapped around it.

'Put the boy in the boat,' said the man without turning.

He spoke with a dismissive rasp, as if he had chosen not to clear his throat first. Although his voice was low, the words whipped through the screams like rain through the cover of night.

Flinching, Mordred peered closer at the thing in his fingers. No bigger than a brooch-pin, it had been looped at the top to make it look a little like a sword or knife. It had to be another umbilical cord. Pressed, twisted, re-shaped. From its lower end droplets fell, staining the sand dark brown. It looked both old and new; as if it had been dripping blood for years, decades.

Mordred's heart beat as high as his throat. He thought he might fall; he couldn't be sure what was keeping him upright. All he felt was an ebbing: of his confidence, his earlier sense of a life shared in peace, even a part of his desire. He was holding himself up by the scruff of his own neck, pressing his nose and lips hard against his farthest limits.

'Whose is that?' he gasped, gesturing at the skin-sword.

'Yours,' came the answer as the hunched man turned at

last, looked up, pushed the sliver between his own parted lips, chewed once and swallowed.

The line of blood that spilled down his chin scarcely showed on his crimson skin. If this single merlin had been cooked from the many, then here by these stones he was still gently simmering. A heat haze rose with the motion of his head, scrambling his features, making his whole curved frame vibrate.

Hopelessly stranded, Mordred took one step back, then lurched forward and kicked out at the cairn in defiance. A sorry little stab of the foot – petulant, not challenging. He had come such a long way to this shore, and still he expected nothing to meet him but misery, fear and confusion.

The tiny tower tumbled, each of its lower stones stained redder than the one just above. Ruined, it lay in a thin pool of quickly drying blood. It was as if the cord had been snapped off like a tendril pushing through from some deep subterranean birthplace.

Man-garden, Mordred thought. Then *Not my blood*. And he smiled at his own sad stupidity: at last he had begun to see what Logres would be. This wasn't a man-garden at all, but a *land*-garden: the seed of a world re-sown and brought back now to fruit.

The child's sound grew inhuman, more like a flock of birds cawing. Mordred thought he felt their wingbeats too; an army of ravens all around him. He turned his gaze back to the hazy face.

Now at least it had settled. Neither old nor young – but also, in truth, neither quite alive nor dead. An effigy with breath, the self-made son of no man. Here was the sum of all the other merlins' parts, but more than that too. He looked less like a person than a principle, not repellent in himself but unreachable on any purely human level.

'The boy,' he repeated, nodding as if to show that already he had a range of movements open to him, then tilting his head to indicate the water. 'In the boat.' When he spoke his large mouth looked serrated.

'Why?' Mordred shouted, but his voice didn't have the same strength against the baby's. 'You won't be taking him anywhere, will you? Logres is going to be here. This will be the coming kingdom – just as it once was the last.'

The ageless man looked down at his shattered stone-pile. The cloak was wrapped so tight around him that the line of his shoulder-blades showed. Mordred knelt, holding the racked child away from him.

'Tell me I'm right,' he pleaded. He slapped the sand with his free hand. 'That it's all in here waiting? Everything, everyone, Logres. It's not just the king who'll come again but his country too. Here. Here!'

The man made no reply, but Mordred didn't need it. This was the only place, the place that was time. One kingdom lay behind it and another lay ahead, but this was the eye of the needle. And Arthur would be the first to pass through it. So many others were waiting from before. Here, here.

'And what about me now?' he roared, narrow-eyed with the effort. 'Will I have what I want now?'

He didn't know why he was asking. He no longer

knew what he wanted. Any earlier bargain seemed irrelevant, struck in laughable ignorance of the inevitable. The kind of deal that the day might have made with the night to stop it from falling.

'Put the boy in the boat.'

'And then what? For me? Tell me!'

The face showed itself again. Their eyes met. Mordred felt as if he weren't looking into just two eyes but a whole peacock-tail's display of them.

'You'll have what you want,' came the reply. It sounded like a sentence.

Mordred stood. He felt too small to carry the once and future king to the skiff, but somehow he managed it. He set it down in a place where the wood was merely damp and not puddled. As soon as he let it go, its roar subsided. Not his son, not his own son.

From the corner of his eye he saw the seven women approaching. Quickly he turned away and made for the cliff-path. He couldn't bear to see what came next. None of it – he knew – would ever bring him peace.

What you want. Which was so little; it had always been so little. Just to share a world. Any world. With anyone who wanted him for who he was, not what.

Half-way up the cliff he thought he heard laughter, but still no sea-sounds. Soon he was back in thin sunlight. There was the villa. There: the ridge on fire behind it. He was crying without the first idea who his tears were for.

Looking down, he saw the armlet on his wrist. He had forgotten to get rid of it with the child. Pulling it off, he twisted round, took two steps back and hurled it with all his strength towards the wall of water.

He didn't look to see if it reached; he didn't need to. Suddenly he heard the sea again, crashing in behind him, swallowing the skiff and child, widening the needle's eye. The sea that was parent to the land, already raising Logres out of Avalon.

Wiping his eyes dry, Mordred walked on.

Part Four

WATER

TWELVE

It hadn't been like the first time.

Second time around, it had all been so different for Morgan. Not easier, but from start to finish the hurts had seemed more remote. Maybe she was just more practised now at keeping herself apart.

It had left her feeling different too. Less bereft than before. She needed no Guenever this time to spell out that it wasn't her own son. It hadn't even crossed her mind. He had no more belonged to her than the steam belonged to the villa's underfloor heating system.

Slowly Morgan rose, gripping the edge of the slab. Moments earlier the fountain inside it had stopped spouting water. Something large was happening around her now — some colossal new end and beginning — but she had little interest in any of that.

She passed from hand to hand Mordred's loincloth, soaked by her tears of bitter relief. It had helped her to cry. Not just because it had blocked her ears to the baby's wails. Perhaps she should have let herself cry more the first time. Then she might not have needed to unleash herself on Mordred's sleeping body. But she doubted it. Fate's hand had been pushing them from start to finish. Pushing or pulling. And a foul, broken-nailed, filthy-fingered thing it was too.

She threw down the cloth. Closing her eyes, she felt spits on her face. It didn't feel like rain – more like sea-spray, or a fine hail from the fountain's main column of water. But the fountain still wasn't working. And when she licked the corner of her mouth, she tasted salt.

Moronoe . . . Mazoe . . . Gliten . . . she started to recite, hoping the string of names might cast a spell to keep it all away from her.

Then she tried to pray, but the older words wouldn't come. Nor would any image of a listening Christ, a merciful God. All she saw inside her head was water. Even when she opened her eyes again, the waves kept crashing in, the tide kept crawling forward openmouthed, spewing up men and their families too: all Arthur's people coming back to find their king . . .

She raised her eyes and saw a bird wing in from the shore and settle on the stained statue. It wasn't a cormorant. No kind of a seabird at all. This was heavier, blacker, almost muscular: a raven.

Morgan's fingers fluttered to her upper arm. It was strange to find no armlet there. Without it she felt undefined. Vulnerable too. Even in front of this bird which seemed to be eyeing her now with such disappointment. She rubbed her bare flesh hard, as if by chafing her own skin she could drive the thing away. But the raven wouldn't move. And in the end Morgan backed into the colonnade, leaving it to preside over the whole sorry scene: broken fountain, spumy drizzle, tear-sodden loincloth and all.

She numbly returned to the room where she slept. The air in there was stale and warm but also, disturbingly, damp with the same kind of invisible spits as outside. At a loss, she went to stand in front of the mirror.

The line of her body had returned to her perfectly. No one would have guessed that she had given birth so recently. The Great Remaking, she thought, and smiled. The cosmetics and brushes she had used to reclaim her face still lay scattered under the glass. She eased them aside with her foot and came closer, fighting to recognize her features through the tear-streaked paint.

Listlessly she wiped the worst of it from her face. Soon, she knew, there would be more mess. Mordred would return and she would have to let him in. A part of her still wanted that. She had to have someone – she had been shown here, beyond all doubt, that she couldn't be alone – and Mordred was as good as any.

There would have to be more sex, but already it was hard to remember quite why. For solace perhaps, or to save themselves from speaking. In their own different ways they had both needed to connect before. Now they would mate to stop the connection from becoming tighter. Make love to maintain the space between them.

'Moronoe . . . Mazoe . . . Gliten . . . Glitonea . . .' she mouthed at the glass.

'. . . Cliton . . . Tyronoe . . . Thitis . . .' a smaller voice continued from the doorway.

Morgan twisted round and saw Anna coming towards her. She knew it was Anna because, under her loose hair, the knife-mark showed white and serpentine against the freckles. She stopped an arm's length away, straight-backed, her hands at her sides as if she were presenting herself for orders, or for a fresh blow to the face.

Morgan reached out to touch the scar. This time the waters had swept the girl back ashore aged twelve or thirteen, pretty as ever, shy-eyed. She could have been a younger, redder Guenever. Anna closed her hand over Morgan's fingers. They stayed locked in this odd, distant embrace for so long that Morgan thought they must have merged.

'Shouldn't you be with the women?' she said in the end.

Anna lifted away her hand. 'Our place is now in Logres.'

Logres. The kingdom that would come. The kingdom made for the king. Morgan shook her head in bewilderment at the girl's barely formed breasts which such a short time before had been brimming with milk. She looked composed but ready to fly away – presumably as soon as she heard Mordred coming back. *If* Mordred came back.

Morgan went to her bed and sank on to it.

'You won't be able to stay here,' Anna said softly, confidentially.

186

Guenever had used exactly the same words after the first birth. She had said them in exactly the same way too. It had been a deliberate echo. This girl was wanting her to hear it. She was trying to make Morgan see something momentous about herself. But Morgan wasn't ready yet.

She frowned at her own reflection rather than at Anna's. Here, she had said; she couldn't stay *here*. 'In this island, you mean?'

'In the villa.'

'I'll have to go back where I came from?'

'This is where you came from. Once it was Albion. Now it will be Logres.' She put out a hand. 'Come with me now. It would be better to come now.'

'Better than what?'

Anna bit on the inside of her cheek and stared back solemnly. Her arm was still held out. Morgan drew up her legs and stretched her own fully extended arms between them. In the mirror she looked as if she were trying to turn herself inside out. And around her a new kingdom was hatching out of the old. Logres was coming. Every moment it came closer.

'Is this the Great Remaking?' she asked distractedly.

Anna nodded. Outside the sea beat louder, burdened now by the living survivors of the deluge that had swamped Albion.

Morgan's face was sleek with the sea's unseeable spray. She smiled at it in the mirror. Her reflection smiled back at her; it looked fuller than before, softer. The glass seemed to be drawing her in, taking her under its surface and reuniting her with her own truest self. Herself into this. Albion into Logres. And Anna – what at last would Anna become, in Logres?

But when she looked up again, Anna had gone. Morgan wasn't entirely sure that she had ever been there.

Mordred saw the girl spinning away down the portico as he approached his mother's room. It looked like one of the shore-women but it could have been Anna. Another member of that strange little Anna nation, each one wearing the Anna-wound in her head. As he watched her leave, she seemed to grow higher. Maybe she was mutating again.

He wasn't surprised. Since hurling the dragon armlet at the water, he had felt a rush around him, a sound like time unleashed. Each step up from the cliff had been harder, as if he were walking through rivers of minutes.

For him, the sea had not retreated. It had swept up over this entire ledge of land, making a far more massive cauldron than before, twisting up time wherever it touched. He put a hand to his jaw. Maybe he too would have aged; his beard might have thinned or fallen out.

But nothing, for him, was different. He knew what he was: the eye of this circling storm, the single pin that held all time's folds together. So many worlds still sat on his shoulder. And still he was so cold. Outside Morgan's room he paused. He felt as if he had come back dripping with the baby's blood, that he had stained every blade of grass between the cliff-top and here.

He didn't know what he would find inside. *Without him, she's yours.* The villa's smell had subtly been changing since he had come in. Wholly feminine, sourer than Morgan's but shot through with hers as well. It hit him higher in the nose, as if it weren't entering through his nostrils so much as descending from his memory.

He stepped into the doorway and looked inside. He shook at what he saw. Morgan's back was to him as she lay on the bed, absorbed in her own mirror image. Those eyes, those eyes. Maybe she could entrance even herself.

Mordred had wondered how she would appear to him now, wondered if all his desire might have been bundled away with the boy in the boat. But he wanted her so badly. Her curved line stirred him straight away. Just the curve, the one svelte line, no particular feature. Icily he burned for her again: a whole pack of animals bristling in heat. The merlins on the shore had converged into a single person. Mordred here was multiplying.

Morgan saw him. She smiled at herself in the mirror. Eyes, eyes. He found himself jealous of her own garish reflection. He didn't want to share her even with a strip of glass. *Without him . . .*

He stumbled forward into the room as if a wave had broken across his back.

Morgan's smile broadened.

He looked young, puffy-eyed. His hands were turned out, little-boy like, as if to show her that he had washed them before his meal. He stood so cowed, waiting to be hit but not knowing if the blow would come from the inside or out.

'It had to happen,' she said without turning to face him.

'To us?'

She watched her own eyes widen. *Us.* It touched her that he saw them as a pair, a couple. But the width of this room was like a world in itself. He was so far away that she could hardly hear his voice.

She shook her head, slowly enough to check both her profiles. In the mirror she saw him moisten his mouth, draw in his lips and show the tip of his tongue. She thought he might be about to cry; she almost hoped he would. If he wept, she would feel able to touch him. Maybe only then.

At last she turned on the bed, rolling on to her stomach and looking up at him like a cat about to spring.

Mordred. Such a sombre name. A name like a weapon put away with the coming of the peace but lying unrusting in the dark, waiting to be taken up again. Because there would always be more war. Wars and kingdoms and stories. Every Age drowned at last in its own sea of blood.

'I love you,' he said from far, far across the world.

It came at her like an accusation. His fingers flexed on the word 'love'. She couldn't imagine he had ever said it to anyone else.

'Can't you speak?' he asked, with an odd new rasp in his voice. She felt as if he had shaken her awake, but she had been unaware of any protracted silence between them. She fixed her eyes on him, but her mind went way past.

The sounds outside were changing. Cries, whinnies, wagon-creaks. They seemed to be coiling out of the nearby water-noise, not rolling down from the ridge or rising from the shore. A world was gathering round her like wool around a spindle. An old world made new.

'I love you,' Mordred repeated.

Although his face looked younger, it seemed sadder too with what it now knew. He stepped up closer, his fingers flexing faster. His right hand brushed the hilt of the knife at his belt. He looked strong above her now, her first mighty child: all the power in his shoulders.

'Come,' she said, easing herself back, then up on to her knees. She smelled burning pitch. She opened her arms. But the shouts outside briefly diverted his attention too.

'Come to me,' she insisted, her arms still outstretched, beckoning him with the tips of her fingers.

He rocked where he stood, but made no move towards her.

She knelt up higher on the bed, so that their eyes were almost level. 'Come,' she urged a third time.

She wasn't sure why she was pressing so hard. Maybe she wanted him more than she was prepared to admit to herself. His fingers had stilled themselves around the hilt of his knife.

He took a single step towards her, then turned sharply as they both heard the thud of bootsteps in the colonnade.

THIRTEEN

Mordred, recoiling, saw the sword before he saw the face. Its holder was waving it so briskly in front of him that he could have been hacking his way through undergrowth.

'Stop!' Morgan called, close to Mordred's back, before the swordsman could come any farther into the room.

Her voice cut through the calls elsewhere in the villa. Soldiers' calls. Urgent, brutish, over-loud. He felt Morgan's breath on his neck.

The soldier paused. '*You?*' he said, narrowing his eyes, but whether at Morgan or himself, Mordred couldn't say.

He felt Morgan move harder against him. She had to be standing on the bed now. Her breasts nestled into the curve of his back, her fingers pressed the backs of his thighs. Mordred quickened all over again.

The swordsman seemed to be peering in disbelief to

either side of his weapon. The moment lengthened and Mordred, almost amused, wondered if he were waiting for him to take out his own little knife in response.

'Put it down,' Morgan said instead. 'You can't touch us here.'

Mordred stiffened. He had never heard her so imperious. And the word 'us' was grimly good. Just her and him, the two of them.

'Lady,' the swordsman answered, 'I am under orders.' He stared up at the tip of his blade as if the thing itself had led him into the room and was continuing to exert its own will. 'We're all moving through now. Every one of us.'

Mordred knew that voice – the way the speaker tried to swallow his words even as he spoke them, as if speech of any kind were a pointless compromise. He looked closer.

The man was big, heavy-shouldered. From the waist down he was glisteningly wet, as if he had waded in from some freshly beached vessel. His thick hair was slicked back from a face that showed regular but relatively small features: a flattish nose, high, clean-shaven cheeks, a pursed mouth circled by a short moustache and beard.

'I know you . . .' Mordred began.

'He's Lanslod,' Morgan sighed into the collar of Mordred's tunic, drawing out the name in a way new to him, pronouncing it rather as 'Lan-ce-lot'.

The smoother-sounding variation suited him better. Mordred's eyes met his and the other man looked away. A man from an earlier kingdom.

Once Lanslod had been Arthur's lieutenant, but obliquely closer to Guenever in that kingdom's last days. Mordred had crossed paths with him at the end: a decent man and doubtless loyal, yet stolid too – limited not only in what he knew but in what he wanted to know. And he looked very different from when Mordred had last seen him. His hair was shorter, his beard less grizzled. His entire physique seemed more finely honed than before. A second chance, Mordred recalled. Would everyone be re-made for Logres?

Morgan was running her fingers down Mordred's spine, lightly pressing each bone, almost as if she expected to find one missing.

'I have been instructed to fetch you, lady,' Lanslod declared with his eyes fixed to the floor. He could have been doing some sort of homage to his own raised sword. Mordred wondered if he had also been instructed to ignore himself. 'As soon as possible now, we must travel inland.'

Morgan's arms snaked around Mordred's waist from behind. She linked her fingers loosely. 'Tell us about it,' she purred.

'Us', again. Even now Mordred basked in this collusion. Maybe it was too late, but the presence of another man seemed finally to be turning their relationship into what it had to be.

'Lady, come,' Lanslod said to a place on the wall just past Mordred's shoulder. 'There will be time for talk later.'

'Where have you come from?' Morgan overrode him. 'Who sent you?'

He shook his head. Mordred glimpsed the uncertainty in his eyes, and for a moment he pitied him. 'Everything is changing,' Lanslod answered, 'and for the better. We have to help to make it change.'

Plainly he was reiterating somebody else's words. He, like all the others outside, must have been swept along by the waters that had covered one kingdom and then raised up another. No words of his own could have made sense of that, least of all to himself.

Morgan's hold on Mordred tightened. She might even have started to rub herself gently against him. Her touch and smell were now so dizzying that he couldn't be sure about anything.

Lanslod tossed his head, indicating the storm of shouts that was sweeping through the villa's rooms and porticoes. 'There are wagons waiting,' he said. 'We can be at court by sunset.'

'Court? Whose court?'

Mordred watched Lanslod back away, as if Morgan had already started to come. Other men rushed past the doorway.

Two tall guards came in, younger than Lanslod, cleaner-shaven, one holding a scentless torch, the other a squat, brutish sword. Like Lanslod himself, they were dressed unlike any soldiers that Mordred had seen before. Their legs and arms were sheathed in what looked like knitted metal; their torsos encased in great iron plates. And they too were wet from wading ashore.

'Whose court?' Morgan repeated coolly. The question sounded like a line from a play in which she had acted far too many times before.

For the first time Lanslod eyed Mordred, not his mother, then looked away. 'Lady,' he said, in palpable confusion, 'you must come.'

But it was Mordred who stepped out into the centre of the room. This haggling had to stop. Lanslod wouldn't be gainsaid; his men would drag her out by force if necessary. And Mordred had to be with her, whether they were planning to take him too or not. He couldn't lose her so soon.

He turned just far enough to catch her wild eye. But when he tried to say, 'We should go,' the words died in his throat.

Feeling faint, he swayed where he stood, buffeted by unseen currents that kept him upright through a momentary fluke of opposition. Currents of water, not air. Deep sea-bed pulses. He felt that he should be looking at the ocean's floor, not at the woman he most wanted to drown inside.

He managed to raise a hand to her, indicating that she should come, but she didn't move an inch. 'Who has given you your orders?' she whispered, almost through Mordred, at Lanslod.

Lanslod flinched. 'The Regent.'

'What Regent?'

Lanslod simply backed again, giving some invisible signal to the pair of guards behind. They surged past him into the room. Mordred drew his knife, intending to spring at whichever came closer. But his new condition made him far too sluggish.

The torch-holder went for Morgan, holding his fiery stump in front of him like an exorcist's cross. He moved fast to Mordred's left, clouded by his own smoke. Simultaneously the other was at Mordred's right side, gripping him surprisingly hard by the upper arm.

Mordred jerked his elbow, but couldn't break free. This was no half-alive merlin, a man he could kill at will. Even as they scuffled fitfully, he felt grateful for that. There had to be an end to all the death.

From the sound of it, Morgan's struggle was equally brief. Then to his surprise she was gliding from behind him towards the doorway, closely followed by the guard with his torch now doused, pausing only to pick up her wrap from a couch as she passed Lanslod.

'Morgan!' Mordred called, letting his own opponent twist his knife-arm so impossibly high behind his back that he felt the blade's tip against his neck.

Outside the room Morgan turned. She looked neither afraid nor outraged; simply submissive to the superior power. 'Everything's changing,' she confirmed, as if Mordred hadn't known that first.

He waited for her to tell the guard to free him, to invite him to accompany her. *We're all moving through now.* But she made as if to shrug, glanced to left and right, then disappeared in the direction of the villa's main entrance.

'*Mother!*' Mordred howled, throwing back his head so that the knife nicked the flesh just below his left ear. He felt absurd, abused – as if he had just been put through a test whose nature and result he would never find out. The guard's grip loosened.

'I want to go with her,' he pleaded hoarsely, hanging his head.

When he looked up, Lanslod was staring at him. 'Haven't you done enough?' the older man asked. His expression was scathing, but it sounded like a genuine question: earnest, sympathetic, as if he were offering Mordred a reprieve, a chance to rest on his laurels at last.

'Please let me be with her.'

Lanslod looked quizzically at the guard, then stepped aside and Mordred felt himself being nudged forward.

He was glad to be guided from the room. Once outside, the guard sensed no fight in him and released his arm. He made no attempt to take the knife. Instead he reached out to where Mordred had been cut and expressionlessly showed him the redness on two of his gloved fingers.

It's not my blood, Mordred thought, but he couldn't spare the energy to say it.

He started to make his own unsteady way to the villa's main entrance. Through the arch he saw the wagons waiting. Not far, not far. But with each step he felt giddier. He felt as if he were breathing in cold, salt water. Everyone around him was moving away from the sea, away from that old drowned world of before; he alone seemed to be heading back towards it.

On the point of struggling out of the building, he collapsed.

Morgan hauled herself aboard the nearest empty vehicle.

A watching guard, as unusually garbed as the others, stepped forward to help her up. She twisted round and widened her eyes at him, which was enough to drive him back in a slither of mail and swordbelt.

The covered wagon wasn't like one of the old kingdom's tribute carts, stinking of animal dung and urine. Benches ran the length of each high wooden side, as if for people to sit on. The wood itself had a different, more polished finish from any that she was used to. Pulling her wrap around her, she sat at the far end, where a heavy brocade curtain separated her from the driver's platform. Then she turned her head and looked out towards the milling cliff-top.

So many guards were swarming. Morgan remembered the old tale of soldiers springing up where a dragon's teeth had been sown. But these were men from the sea, not a new crop from the man-garden: all those who had been riding the deluge that had ended Arthur's Albion.

Bewildered-looking families were herded up from the shore into the wagons. Reprieved at last from the sea, some of the women clutched babies and led children by the hand. None could have known what this new land held for them, but even the men were moving through subdued. The guards themselves were gentle. All the words that Morgan caught were encouraging.

She couldn't feel surprised. It seemed so natural now. All this had been waiting, just as Arthur had been waiting inside Mordred. All of it. Even this fine, salty mist – as real and unseeable outside the villa as it had been inside. *Everything is changing*. And so fast. It must have started as soon as the child had been handed over.

Logres coming, Logres coming . . . Already the land looked more sturdy around her: darker and sharper where once she had thought it so fluid. The round-up continued, but Mordred didn't appear as she had expected he would. Perhaps from this point on, the two of them would be making different journeys. Perhaps they had never really been travelling together at all.

The bustle near the cliff's edge briefly cleared. A long-haired figure in a black hooded cloak – *the* black hooded cloak? – appeared at the head of the path. He stood sideways on to all the activity, but Morgan had a strong impression of the features behind his dark hang of hair. Reptilian yet canine too, he reminded her of every merlin she had ever seen, but with infinitely greater presence. *The* merlin, as it were.

He beckoned to a new shipload of incomers that appeared at the head of the cliff-path, directing them all to the wagons. It seemed outlandish, but Morgan wondered if this was in fact Lanslod's 'Regent', the man who had given him orders.

Then Anna stepped up next to him. She was too far away for Morgan to hear what she said, but she appeared to be speaking fast while looking past him out at the water. He in turn seemed to be straining his upper body away from her where he stood. He took a step back and she turned to glare at him, her hands clamped on her slim hips in Guenever's distinctive style. Finally she moved away and out of sight. The other turned to leave in the opposite direction.

The wagon heaved as its driver climbed up into position. 'Lady,' said a voice from the open end, 'the first convoy will leave now.'

She twisted round to see Lanslod on a pale horse which had been fitted with awesome protective armour on the head and back. What kind of enemies did they think they might have to deal with?

The driver cried out to his horses, but just before they moved Lanslod raised a gloved hand and pointed inside the wagon. 'In here?' he asked, awaiting an instruction from someone out of view. Then he nodded.

Two guards rushed up and between them flung in what looked like a sack of provisions. After a moment, the baggage moaned and groggily pushed itself up on to all fours.

It was Mordred. Bleeding in streams from the neck. But he was losing more than blood.

FOURTEEN

Mordred could feel himself growing backwards: the man ebbing out, the child bursting through to flood its former ground.

Although he was still bleeding, the blood seemed to spill from some other body, from some other kingdom from which only he could not escape. He felt no pain; just the splintery friction inside his skin of time being dragged against its own grain.

Trembling, he put out a hand to Morgan as the wagon gathered speed. She started, holding her wrap tighter around herself. She drew up her knees too, as if she expected the blood to flood across the floorspace and soak her feet.

Mordred pushed himself back onto his knees. Loosely he still held out one hand; the other he pressed to the wound in his neck. It's not my blood, he mouthed at her, too tormented to use his voice. He saw that she had understood. He shook his head at her. Not mine, not mine . . .

But she wouldn't take his hand, didn't dare to touch him. Her fears were surely misplaced. She couldn't change in the same way as him. She would be remade, not unmade. Logres was coming, and already she was passing through the needle's eye that would take her there. He could see it.

Already her skin was taking on the same almost-godly sheen as Lanslod's and the guardsmen's. Her hair had a startling lustre. However splendid she had been before, her beauty was now being improved. Mordred wanted her so badly. None of his need had gone. He craved her woman's hands on his face and legs, her red lips hard against his own.

Storm-tossed, seaborne, he ripped off his tunic's sleeve to staunch the wound. Morgan wouldn't help in any way. The body of his tunic fell, to show a chest as matted as before but with hair less than half its previous length. The horses' hooves drummed towards the ridge, up smooth roadways that had not existed an hour before.

His knife's nick had punctured much more than his skin. *Logres is waiting . . . We'll find it through you . . .* Not just through his re-conception of its future king. Logres was coming through the fabric of his own body. One man as the crucible for a kingdom. A man giving birth to a world.

He lurched around to see how far they had come.

Their wagon was the last in this train. Lone riders brought up the rear – riders and horses like monstrous worms in iron cocoons. Galloping, they rattled louder than all the wagons' shafts, wheels and axles. Headgear hid their faces: helmets shaped like great beaked dogs, sheathed swords at their sides like extensions of themselves.

The ridge receded behind them. The territory to either side had risen from Avalon's mists, a landscape in the making, but the string of beacons' smoke still coarsened the new day's brightness. This land looked less provisional with every passing moment.

The first settlement on their route had seemed unfinished, as if each structure in it could have been scalped down or fleshed out even as Mordred watched. But two of the wagons had turned off into it, and at once all its lines became fixed. The same happened at the next village, then the next. It was like an invasion in reverse: a kingdom being peopled – enhanced and not despoiled by the wide-eyed new arrivals.

And the road was still unfurling only yards ahead of the horses' hooves. The harder they rode, and the further they journeyed, the bigger this kingdom became. One boundary was always just before them, the one behind grew ever more distant. And only the sea would stop their progress in the end. With hooves and wheels and Mordred's own drying blood, they were painting the long-promised land on this space.

Mordred felt moved to be seeing it. A second chance, a new beginning, a truly great re-making. For the first time since leaving Albion, he had travelled out of sight of the sea. But he hadn't left the waters behind. They clashed and coursed around him, stripping him down like a high wind stripping branches. These waters would always be with him, waiting to drown him on the driest of land.

He turned back around to his mother, beseeching her with his eyes.

His need for her made him breathless. Doglike, he padded forward. His head dropped against her thigh. She let out a cry of alarm, but mercifully she didn't try to kick him away or draw up her legs. The smell of her filled his head and groin.

'I want to be inside you,' he choked. 'Just want to be inside you . . .'

The words came out so mangled that even he barely understood them. He closed his eyes but then he felt her hand, tentative against the back of his head.

He wanted to weep, to call her mother. His lips fell apart against the lap she made for him at last. She was holding the rag to his neck for him. It was she, not he, who was sighing at the enormity of it all. Her hand was at his naked back, counting down the vertebrae.

The wagon tore on into the unimaginable interior. Mordred let himself lose consciousness.

There was one brief halt to change the horses. Then they resumed: a handful of wagons now with the riders beside them.

Slowly, mile by mile, Morgan began to recognize the route. She had travelled it before. In both directions as well: to the court, away from the court. There was only one court, whatever the name of the kingdom where it lay.

Whatever Anna had said to the contrary, this was undeniably a homecoming. Morgan knew the great westward-rolling plain so well. The clusters of homes looked much finer than she remembered; plaster in place of twigs, brick instead of mud. Everything else, in essence, was the same.

Here was a kingdom refurbished. A kingdom remade for a king. One king. She closed her eyes and saw him in the darkness: more than a mere black cross, a king like a hook of hardened flesh, coming like a sword lodged in stone, its hilt inside him, its tip about to enter her . . .

She knew that the court – when it came – would sit on a conical hill rising like a tumour from this flatness. 'Camlann' the merlins had called it before. This wasn't a transit of Avalon; they were riding back to Camlann.

During a second, longer halt at a staging post, again Morgan stayed in the wagon. With each passing mile she had grown more tired: a deep and helpless weariness. And she didn't dare shift Mordred off her. At least now he seemed to have stabilized.

For miles, though, she had thought he was dead. He had spilled enough blood for ten and his bones too had been pared down, his sheer bulk diminished. At last she peeled back the crimson rag. There was no sign of a cut on his smudged livid skin. She kissed him then, high on his temple.

New horses were being hitched. Through the curtain, the driver passed back to Morgan a flagon of wine and a plate of hot peppered chops. The meat looked good – her first since coming ashore. But Morgan had no appetite for food or drink. She set them down on the bench beside her, then made a weak grab at his mailed wrist:

'Is this Logres?'

He stared back nonplussed, as if she had spoken in a foreign language.

'Please say.' Smiling, she tugged feebly at his arm, almost hitting Mordred's tousled head with her elbow. 'Tell me where we are. Tell me what you think you're doing.'

'I know enough if I know that I am the king's subject,' he recited.

'Which king?'

'My king. Yours. The king who will come from the water behind us.'

She felt Mordred stir, gripping her haunches tighter. She shut her eyes, felt the phantom sword-tip's brush. *The king from the water.* She saw once more the great galley which had merged with the barge.

Mordred moved again. He twisted his uncut neck and Morgan looked down into his eye. The driver stared from one to the other, then at his wrist which Morgan held white-knuckle tight.

'King Arthur?' murmured Morgan's son into the silence. It sounded more like an answer than a question, an attempt to put her mind at rest.

The driver narrowed his eyes, then nodded. She let go of his wrist and he turned back to his horses.

'Arthur,' a new voice confirmed at the wagon's open end.

Morgan swung around to find the figure from the cliff-top standing there.

Only his head and shoulders were visible, but he looked, if anything, more spectral closer to than from a distance. Maybe Morgan's tired eyes were tricking her, but he didn't seem to have the same veneer as all the others, including even Lanslod.

From here his face wasn't like any man's she had ever seen. It seemed to cover a much bigger proportion of the head than was usual. Neither old nor young, alluring nor repellent – or perhaps all four at once – he seemed to hover outside specific description. Even his hair looked like many men's grafted together: made up of countless shades and textures of darkness.

'Arthur,' he said again, holding her gaze in a flinty kind of challenge. 'There can be no other king. These men are taking possession of the land in his name.'

As he spoke, the driver's curse rang out and the wagon jolted into motion.

At first the face at the far end got no smaller. Morgan imagined that he was standing on an exposed axle, and would be with them now for the rest of the journey. He smiled into her eyes.

'Who are you?' she breathed at him. 'The "Regent"? Is that what you say?'

Still he smiled. 'Think of me as Arthur's Man,' he answered evenly. 'Call me Merlin.'

The wagon gathered speed, but Morgan's mind wouldn't move.

'Logres is coming,' he promised. 'A better kingdom. There will be a place in it for you . . .'

Morgan looked away and held Mordred closer. *For you . . .* But not, she understood, for him; not for the son who had spawned it. He hadn't even looked in Mordred's direction. Merlin. When she looked up again he had disappeared.

She could feel Mordred's teeth through the fabric of her gown, as cold as all the rest of him. He had wanted to be inside her. She closed her eyes, needing to see no more.

They came to the hill's base at sunset.

The wagon tilted sharply as they started their ascent. The uneaten food and undrunk wine slid quickly down the bench and smashed on to the winding track below.

Mordred had hardly moved since falling against Morgan hours before, but he hadn't been unconscious all the time. Through the corner of one eye he had glimpsed some stretches of their route, but none of that mattered – not as much as his closeness to this woman. And he knew she needed to nurse him now as much as he needed to be nursed. The name of Arthur had hit her hard. She was hiding inside herself from what it might mean.

When they drew up under the towering gatehouse, he lifted himself off her. She didn't try to hold him back. Her eyes were wide, red with tears and tiredness, glued to the road that stretched back across the twilit, treeless plain.

Mordred felt less choppy waves around him now. He knelt in front of her, taking her hands in both of his. Her gaze remained fixed, as if she expected a pursuing army to erupt over the dimming horizon. Or just one pursuer. *The king from the water.*

Mordred continued to flag, but he wanted to rally himself for her. He longed to draw new strength from her stupor.

He could see some of the men calling to each other outside the wagon. Glancing up, he saw the hilltop fort that soared above its lower curtain wall. He had never seen a stronghold like it, even though the hill itself was identical to the one on which Arthur's old crude camp had been perched.

This fabulous fort with its towers and buttresses seemed to have been carved from a single block of sandy stone. Gleaming almost golden in the dusk, it had to be the heart of the kingdom coming through. Not so much rising up from the past or seeping back from the future as descending from heaven above, draped across this hilltop like a gorgeous curtain of stone and tile.

He could hear the other vehicles being cleared: guards patiently suggesting that the people inside should step down. Several armed men passed the end of their own wagon but none looked in, none spoke.

'We shouldn't be here,' Morgan whispered, each semi-swallowed word sounding slick with fear.

Mordred took her two forefingers and rubbed them gently with his thumbs. 'We' was wrong. The wagon juddered. The draught-horses stepped on through the opened gates and up the steep path to the city from the sky.

They passed their fellow-travellers, who were striding wonderingly up the incline in knots. Smoke coloured the early-evening air. Mordred saw its swirls of ash but he smelled no fires, no pitch from any torch, no roasting meat. This was a world not meant for him. The membranes were closing over him like a mist closing over the moon. Already he was on his way out. Like an unbaptized baby, he had never fully entered this world in the first place. Now he was going back while everyone else went forward.

Still holding Morgan's forefingers, he eased himself to his feet. He was shorter than before – only by an inch or two, but his eyes felt so much closer to his feet. He knew it had still hardly started. The first warning gust of a storm that would blow him right away. And nothing he did could save him now. Afraid though he was, there was nowhere to hide. He felt so sick at what he would miss, but he couldn't fit through this needle's eye.

He let go of his mother. His tunic had flapped down, leaving his blood-streaked body bare above the belt. Since he had no underclothes he ripped off its top portion, turned aside, then looped and tied it between his legs. His erection had returned as soon as he had touched Morgan's fingers.

'Don't leave me now,' she said softly, staring into his groin.

He bent to kiss the crown of her splendid head: the truest queen he had ever seen.

At the top of the slope, the darkness of the higher gatehouse closed around them. The wagon stopped for the last time.

'They can walk from here,' said a voice Mordred recognized.

With Morgan now pressing her head against his thigh, he turned to watch the speaker appear at the back of the wagon.

FIFTEEN

Morgan had distinctly heard Guenever speak. But there stood Anna, still a girl in puberty, twirling a length of red hair around one of her fingers.

Morgan watched her from the wagon. She had always seen the girl and queen as close: like Mordred and herself, two shouts in the same silence. But she had to accept now that this was different. These two women were echoes of each other, maybe in some way that involved the other seven too. *Moronoe . . . Mazoe . . . Gliten . . . Glitonea . . .*

Anna smiled from the gatehouse gloom. Farther inside the court, bells tolled rhythmically. 'Welcome to Camelot,' she said in a voice half-way between Guenever's and her own; it sounded uncannily like a younger version of the heron-woman's outside the villa. And Camelot now, Morgan noticed, not Camlann. 'Come down.'

'It's you, isn't it?' In her alarm Morgan's own voice sounded high and thin. Mordred drew her closer to his icy, bloodied leg. 'You're the same person. You have been all along. You're Guenever.'

Anna's smile narrowed. 'You'll have everything you need here,' was all she said. Then she drifted into the dark multitude, expecting them to follow. Morgan watched the blue of her dress grow dimmer as she moved away.

'We have to go,' Mordred wheezed, helping her to her feet.

His steadiness stunned Morgan. She remembered him falling into the wagon at the villa. Even then she had thought that she could hear the crack of his bones as they contracted. Certainly she had seen his first few premature anxiety lines smearing themselves off his face. And that blood. So much blood. If time was an arrow, then for Mordred it was hurtling back to its original quiver now. But his obliviousness to his own ordeal seemed so noble.

'Come,' he coaxed, already outside and raising his arms to her.

She let him take her weight, he staggered, and she fell heavily against him. He was hard inside his makeshift loincloth. As if to reassure her, he kissed her hair. *Moronoe . . . Mazoe . . .* She shut her eyes, distraught, and saw the greater evil lumbering after them, big enough again to walk through the water all around this land. Armed with only himself, spilling his shadow on before him to swallow every light.

'I'm with you,' Morgan whispered into the raw cold

of Mordred's uncut neck, barely audibly above the bells' din. 'I'll stay with you.'

The guards stalked around them, all Arthur's Men, taking possession of the land, manning these walls that would stand at its centre.

Mordred coiled his limp arm around her waist and fastened his hand to her hip. The fine salty drizzle from the villa hung on the air here too. Together they passed through the gatehouse behind the distant Anna.

Morgan's first sight of Camelot made her catch her breath.

The paths through Arthur's brutish fort in the kingdom had followed the same design. But blackened wooden huts had lined the ways there. Here the courtiers' homes were great slabs of barely weathered stone, all as elegant as the villa. Arthur's verges had been strewn with animal dirt and piles of putrid cuts of beasts inedible even by him. Here, beneath the high pennanted towers, fruit trees spiced the evening air.

Everything is changing. Logres was so close; Morgan could feel its breath on her neck, its damp sea-gestation on her face.

Mordred, she knew, felt it too. His step was horribly uneven and five times he stumbled. Not through losing his footing – the ground was as smooth here as Morgan's own skin. He was being buffeted from beyond the walls. Scythed by the oncoming shadow: his own child turned back into man.

His grip on her hip tightened. He needed her support now more than she needed his. Fresh cuts showed on his side, in exactly the same places where Morgan had first thought she saw them at the villa. Fat slashes in his skin, inflicted from some unthinkable distance but still striking rivulets of blood.

'It's not mine,' he told her hoarsely, wrenching them both forward. The more blood that showed, the thinner grew the drizzle. And, Morgan noticed, the slower tolled the bells.

The palatial hall loomed above them, ringed by stiff-backed guards. Anna, unchallenged, was already ascending its wide flight of steps.

Morgan was too traumatized to cry. The blood wasn't his. It wasn't for him either, it was all for this new kingdom. And everyone around them seemed to have acknowledged that. None of the bells rang any more. Each man, woman and child now drew back to take stock of the beautiful black-haired youth who was bleeding his height and shedding his strength, but only for them.

Morgan reached over and pressed his wounds with the bunched end of her wrap. The pelt on his chest had thinned; he was no taller now than she was.

The bustle had ceased in the concourse, and up on the battlements too. Step by step, Mordred had drawn them into his drama: which was their own drama, distilled to the scale of a single person. All the hurts of the Great Remaking were being painted on to his flesh. Morgan felt as if she were escorting him to his own martyrdom; yet still he was trying to carry her like his cross.

'Don't let me fall,' he mouthed into her ear. His voice

was weaker but no less deep than before. 'Don't let me drop in front of them.'

She held him close, dabbing at him with her free hand. But she knew that the steps would be too much. There were thirty, maybe forty of them. Anna had slowed as she came to the top.

'Help us!' Morgan shrieked up at the girl. '*Help* us.'

Slowly, gracefully, Anna turned and smiled. She looked huge in the fading torch-tinged daylight. Monumental; sculpted from the same stone as the city. She put a hand to her forehead, absently pushing back her hair to show the telltale tuck in her skin. It seemed to Morgan to be as big as Mordred now, a gash that could swallow him whole. She stared up at it, into it, and saw the seas of blood swilling beneath.

'He can't be helped,' Anna called back down. 'Not here. This place is not for him.'

Morgan turned Mordred and pressed him against her, front to bleeding front like a body shield. He twitched as new blows surprised him, scarred him. Morgan couldn't keep them off. And still his sheared-down penis was stiff. He still had a man's mind – and a man's memory – inside his own blood.

Morgan pushed his face into her neck and glared up over his head. *Cliton . . . Tyronoe . . . Thitis . . .* She felt as if she were looking up at all seven of the women from the shore alongside Anna. And they were merging, like the merlins before them, into some new shape altogether.

'Has it always been you?' she cried up at Anna, her question striking echoes off the tableau of splendour all around. 'Always, from the start, making all this happen . . .'

Anna shook her head. 'I'm part of something larger.'

'You're Guenever. I know you.'

Anna's stone smile widened. She spread her stone arms. It looked like a ritual gesture, a call to prayer, although Morgan had no idea what kind of a god she might be invoking. All she could hold in her mind was the steps, her son in convulsions, the coming of the shadow.

Then Anna simply beckoned, curling the fingers of both hands. 'Come . . .'

You'll have everything you need here. Not one hushed onlooker came out to lend a hand. Morgan hadn't expected it. They weren't really here; not yet. They hadn't fully turned into themselves. Just as Anna wasn't quite yet Guenever. And finally, in this as in so much else, Morgan knew that she had no choice.

She shuffled Mordred, stooped, then hoisted his poor pierced frame into her arms. Holding him under his arms and knees, she set off.

He smiled thinly into her face as they went higher. After ten steps he shut his eyes. He looked as if he had slipped under the surface of a stretch of stilled water. His hair fanned around his head although no wind blew. His blood and cuts faded as if unseen hands were washing them off.

He looked so peaceful that Morgan let herself weep. But still she struggled up.

As soon as she had lifted him, he stopped sinking. No

218

longer drowning on dry land; now he swam in the sundown stone.

In an earlier deluge, pairs of the world's creatures had been saved. Not here. On this stairway there was one pair going nowhere. Away from nothing, towards nothing. Avalon had been their Ark; but all that existed in this new bloated moment was Morgan, himself and the steps.

He needed to sleep. To wrap it all around as a dream. Sleep to give it shape and distance. But no sleep came. He thought he sensed the presence of the women from the shore. Sirens who made no sound. Sirens without a song. Now there was nothing but water. The mighty waves were ruling all again. And his mother was his barge, keeping him afloat for just a little longer.

He felt no proper anger. He saw no malice in the way that they had used him. As before, he had served a good purpose. His life had never been his own but a part of something larger. First a larger darkness, but here – in time – a brighter light.

Round and round he span, tighter inside the flesh that buoyed him up. He felt like a part of some other, huger person. But all the persons here were him, all the possible Mordreds. And only one would go on. Only one would be snatched at and lifted. Already he saw the hand descend.

He knew it from before: big below his waist, gripping him by the groin and hauling him high. He screamed, but no sound came. No sound would have mattered anyway.

Mordred felt the light inside himself dim. The darkness seeped up and he was taken.

'Set him down there. On one of the couches. Please.'

The voice was female, imperious but warm. Morgan looked from side to side through her tears. Whoever had spoken was hiding herself. Morgan felt no need to obey. The load in her arms had lost its weight as they had risen. And the thinner Mordred grew, the more she had wanted to keep him.

'He doesn't need you any more,' came the voice again, warmer still. 'He sleeps. Let him rest here.'

Here. Morgan looked around herself.

Incense burned cloudily in braziers. Two trees of short candles shed a furtive, anaemic light. She had expected a grand feasting hall, but inside the gated arch at the top of the temple-like steps she had entered this pool chamber.

It was much the same size as the one at the villa. But whereas at the villa half a dozen couches had stood by the water's edge, here the pool's entire perimeter was surrounded by a circle of them. It was as if all the empty upholstered benches were forming a barrier.

Morgan stepped up to the nearest, sat by the head-rest and laid Mordred out with his face in her lap. The water was mirror-still, but the room was full of spray. Sodden already, her own clothes clung to her. It was as if great waves were crashing just out of sight, but sending on this spindrift.

She ran her hands down Mordred's now-cleaned spine

The hair on him was slightly less dark than before, though just as dense. His knife was still in his belt, seeping blood of its own almost imperceptibly into the couch's rich fabric. Morgan fingered its hilt, wrapped around with the horny cord. But she didn't dare to take and hurl it into the water. It was his. It went with him, like one of his limbs.

'You can't save him,' commiserated the voice from much closer. 'Not here.'

'Why?' Morgan turned him and let her spinning head drop so low that her hair coiled over his chest. 'Why can I never? Why do I always have to lose him?'

A hand touched her shoulder, light, unthreatening. 'He's not your son. Not just your son. And this is a world not meant for him. His seed was sown in darkness. Here, without him, there can be only light.'

Morgan pressed her face into Mordred's shrunken rib-cage. She felt as if she were still climbing the steps. She could have carried him all the way up to Christ's heaven, where the waves would never scar him. Her child was so hideously out of his element here.

'Put him back in the water,' coaxed the voice. 'It's where he came from; where he must return – for your sake as well as for his own.'

Morgan felt her heart contract. '*Drown* him?' The word caught in her throat and came out like a howl.

'*Save* him, from what would be worse.'

The hand soothed her as the words worked their confusion. Guenever's hand; it had to be hers. Once it might have been Anna's – or even one of the other seven's – but with the king now so close, this could only be his waiting wife. *Part of something larger.* Guenever came with this kingdom as she had come with the last.

And for Morgan that meant more torment. She hadn't found it hard to keep Anna at arm's length. The childless older woman touched her closer: her saviour yet her rival too, releasing her from webs of fate spun surely by herself. Already, as ever in her presence, Morgan felt gauche, dwarfed, outnumbered. And she wouldn't see Guenever as queen, not even here. *There can be no other king*, the figure who called himself Merlin had rightly said. But there was only one true queen as well: the one to whom the brute ruler had gone by nature, the sister who had made him his baby.

'I love him now,' she whispered, more to herself than to Mordred or to Guenever, whose fingers flexed on her shoulder. 'I can't let him go again.'

'Logres is coming,' the island's first lady reminded her. 'The kingdom made for the king. This child can't be there. The king will want him; he'll want you because of him . . .'

Morgan had stopped hearing. Shrugging off the hand, she drew Mordred's tunic up over his belt. His makeshift loincloth had sagged to one side and his penis, still engorged, thrust out from under it. A sleek little sea-slug in strands of dark ocean grass.

Not just your son. It gave Morgan gooseflesh to think what that meant.

Holding back her hair, she closed her mouth over him His wintry pubic range came inside her lips. I love you she thought as her tongue flicked his glans. He wasn't her son. Not yet. He had wanted to be inside her. No one could stop that now. Not even Guenever, whose footsteps Morgan heard softly receding.

She put her hand over the seeping blade to stop it from touching her breast. Then she worked faster at Mordred with her tongue. Just the gentlest suggestion of pressure.

She closed her eyes and there was no one in pursuit. However briefly, this protracted kiss was dragging her out of the king's oncoming shadow. She *was* still climbing the steps with her baby. Higher, higher; through this chamber's roof, faster through the night sky until they were stepping past the stars, the misted-over moon, the seas that stormed behind it all . . .

He came in a single spasm.

Morgan gripped him with her lips and moved her head in tiny circles until no more of the tartness ran down her throat. She had taken the last of the man out of him. Now, truly, he had become her son. She kept her eyes closed, and still there was no king.

Another hand closed on her shoulder. It felt like a talon.

'Now,' said a male voice above her, 'end it.'

SIXTEEN

Morgan opened her eyes. She saw the streak of red a
Mordred's groin and, putting her fingers to her mouth
she found crimson there too.

'He comes in blood,' the grimly familiar male voic
sounded again.

Morgan twisted round, spit-mixed blood flicking fron
her lips as she stood. The figure in the black hoode
cloak smiled back. Merlin. His eyes, although wide an
surprisingly bright, hid much more than they showed
He stood around the pool's corner, rangy and slightl
stooped, resting some of his sinewy weight against
couch. His face now had almost no colour, his skin wa
unwrinkled too, yet he looked antique, like those statue
in stone in the courtyard at the villa. With his strong
hooked nose and sensual mouth he might have passe
for one of the giants who had carved them. But surel
unlike the giants of old, his manner was almost effete.

'He has never been truly alive here,' he went on. 'There can be no place for him. He's meant to be dead.'

'Meant. Meant!' Morgan lurched forward, intending to fly at him in spite of her tiredness. He sounded like every merlin she had ever heard: portentous, narrow, forcing the truth in advance into tales. Even when there had been scores of them, they had only ever spoken with a single voice.

But a hand closed high on her arm from behind; the arm where once she had worn Arthur's dragon armlet. Briefly the fingers seemed to be feeling for it through the wrap. Morgan swung around to find herself facing Guenever.

It was too much. Morgan fell against her in a choked embrace, burying her face in the gossamer blue-grey gown, as wet as Morgan's own. As Guenever murmured wordless consolations, Morgan slumped in her arms; she barely felt able to stand. Fatigue was spreading from her eyes outward.

When Guenever prised their bodies a short way apart, there was just enough space between them for little Mordred to have stood inside their linked arms. Perhaps that was where they should have kept him from the start. All on the same side, a common front against the king.

Guenever swallowed. Calm, pale, her prominent features were accentuated by tightly swept-up hair. The gold band at her neck made her look misleadingly vulnerable. She was beautiful, but in a way that only other women really appreciated. A beauty seen clearest through envy; a calmness made compulsive by the fact that it could never be one's own. She was so many women to Morgan. And every woman, in a sense, was Guenever. All the women that Arthur didn't need to be with.

She released one of Morgan's arms, gathered the loose sleeve of her own gown and put it to Morgan's mouth. 'You had blood there,' she explained, exerting gentle pressure on her lips.

Morgan looked into her dark eyes. They urged her not to speak. Guenever had never had much time for words. In that, at least, she had been suited to Arthur. But Morgan needed to talk. As long as she spoke, she wouldn't surrender to sleep – and to the nightmare that must follow.

'I love him now,' Morgan repeated, with a nod towards the sleeper.

Guenever tilted her head. Her azure pendant earrings swayed.

'Why did you ever let him live?' Morgan pleaded. 'Why did you save him the first time?'

'Because he was needed.' This answer came from the man behind Morgan. Merlin: the ultimate Land Man. The fruit of all that carnage on the shore. Guenever looked at him, and Morgan saw repugnance in her eyes.

'After his birth,' Guenever went on to Morgan, 'and with you gone, so much changed. Arthur went . . inside. He lived like the beast he had always been – in a pit dug under the court, where Bran's head was said to have been buried.' She tried to smile; but her smile

226

like snow, had always both cleansed and covered. She gestured at Mordred, 'And then, in the end, the child came back . . .'

'Back in blood,' the man behind Morgan put in, 'just as we said he would.'

We. He was trumpeting his origins. Again Guenever's eyes flashed. She touched the gold at her wrist, then dampened her lips impatiently with the tip of her tongue. The faint red stain on her sleeve looked huge.

Morgan glanced back at the couch. The mist in the room had thinned. New contusions showed on Mordred's legs and chest, blacker bruises, stripped-back slivers of skin. He was bleeding from his ears and nose as still he shrank. There were stains on the couch where his feet no longer reached. He wasn't much bigger now than Anna when Morgan first had seen her.

Clutching at the place where her armlet used to be, she stepped back to him and knelt. She kissed the crown of his head, stroked his hairless arm.

'How could you ask me to drown him?' she said incredulously over her shoulder. But she knew that it hadn't been a genuine request; just a challenge that both Guenever and maybe Merlin too had never expected her to meet. It was almost as if they were covering themselves against what must then happen instead. 'Would you have wanted me to fish him out after?'

'The pool is bottomless,' Merlin replied for her. 'The water is salt. Whatever enters it goes back to the ocean, back to the beginning.'

Morgan turned. He was edging between two of the

couches, then he squatted by the pool. She saw him hitch up his cloak, dip one slender foot in the water, and start to describe circles with it. In her lethargy she felt drawn to the ripples – doubtless as he had known she would be. But she managed to rouse herself. There was just a chance that she could turn to her own advantage the tension between the two others.

Morgan rose and crossed back to Guenever. Still she felt as if she were ascending the steps. She had to keep talking, keep moving. She put her hands on Guenever's and squeezed them; they felt so warm after Mordred.

'Help me,' she whispered. 'Help us.' But she couldn't escape Merlin's range of hearing. For all the tension between them, he was closer to Guenever than Morgan had ever been. There was no single Regent here, but both of them: Land Man and Water Woman, each incomplete without the other.

'It's too late,' he called. 'The cord to the last kingdom must be cut.'

Morgan looked back. No evening light now spilled through the open doorway. In the candles' soft shimmer he looked waxen; as if he were about to topple into the pool and slowly spread across every inch of its surface. Water, always water. And Morgan knew what he meant by 'the cord': Mordred. Her son had brought this world out of the other. Fed it through himself. But although he had once been so vital, he could now be tossed aside.

'He will be a worthy king,' Merlin pronounced, as if by rote. 'An Arthur to be revered, flesh on the bones of the dream from before.'

'It will be a second chance,' Guenever corroborated. She pulled out a hand from under Morgan's and clasped hers in turn. 'There has to be sadness but good will follow. The better part of your son will live on in the king. This time it will be different.'

Merlin smiled grimly. 'Not a kingdom this time, but an empire. Its glory will be fanned into the corners of the earth!'

'Words! More stories!' Morgan longed to sink to her knees and sleep.

'Words make worlds,' Merlin spat back. 'In the beginning was the word, and in the end as well. Men simply pass in the middle. The word is made flesh, then turns back into word. Why mistrust stories? They outlast us all.'

Guenever pulled her back round. 'It has to be different. A different kingdom. A new beginning. For all of us. For all those outside. Like you now, they're ready for better.'

'And isn't he too?' Morgan waved a bone-weary arm back towards Mordred.

Speak, move. She was crawling up the steps now; Mordred was strapped to her back; hand above hand, hauling herself higher. But the shadow was close to her heels. 'Without him you couldn't have your Logres and your Camelot,' she tried to argue. 'Why should he be the sacrifice? He was just the proof of what was wrong before, not its cause.'

'He can't be here when the king comes again.' Guenever's words flew at her like weights; their impact drove her to her knees. 'But you will have a place of dignity. You will never be touched again. Not in the old way.'

Morgan was static on the stairway. It was as if another body had grown around her, stultifying movement. She waited to hear the waters break to take her slandered son. If they truly wanted him drowned, then surely they would tip him in themselves. She clasped her hands as if to pray.

'Now,' Guenever coaxed her, 'put him where he has to be. Logres will be built on him, on his better blood.'

Morgan raised her eyes to the woman who soared above her: the spoil of Arthur's victory in the wars. The woman that he had been given, but never the one that he took. The king's own coming in the wartime had quickly passed into legend. *Cometh the hour, cometh the man*. Guenever's coming at the peace had been so much quieter. Only Morgan had been suspicious. Now nothing but childbirth seemed beyond her. She might even have spawned the wars in the first place, just to find an Arthur to end them. To find him for herself. And here in the end, beside Merlin, she was giving birth to a whole new world.

'Does it have to be like this?' Morgan begged. 'Does it always?'

'Did you bemuse the king into loving you?' Merlin asked her back.

Morgan stared up tearfully into her rival's eyes. She didn't know the answer any more, just the story. The

230

authorized line that would live on for ever. 'Only if you made me.'

She was sliding down the steps. The shadow flickered, hot on her back. She drew in her breath and heard the small flat slop of the water's surface being split. Slowly she twisted her neck. Ripples reached out from the centre: darker than the water at the edge. Blood-dark in the candles' glow. Then, straining her eyes through a fresh storm of spray, she saw . . .

Mordred's smeared knife lay half-immersed. Its strangely acute angle suggested that it was being held from below, by the blade. As Morgan watched, the hilt's wrapping uncoiled across the surface, seemed to throb, then swam away like a serpent into the depths. At once the knife was tilted vertical: an inch or two of the blade showed above the water as well as the bare bone hilt. Then down it plunged and out of sight.

A delighted hand-clap shattered the silence.

Morgan turned the other way, to where the sound came from. Mordred – the size of a four-year-old, naked, unscathed – was standing at the pool's edge, his tiny toes curled over its rim. He clapped again, grinning at his mother. Then he showed her what he had done, mimicking the motion of his own chubby arm when he had flung the murderous thing into the pool.

Aghast, Morgan hoisted herself to her feet. Neither Guenever nor Merlin moved. Mordred wheeled his arm again. His re-grown mane flew up in the back-draught.

231

'Knife,' he said with glee. 'Not my blood.' And then, peering down as a gap-toothed grin opened up his face: 'Father . . .'

Morgan raised her eyes in exhaustion and saw the endless stairway tapering up to the sky.

'Come,' she called across to him, beating her thigh as if he were a dog. She fought through her torpor, back towards the doorway. The child pouted at her, stared again at the water, wouldn't obey.

'Come now,' Morgan implored him.

Her words echoed loudly back at her. Merlin and Guenever were like statues; neither seemed to be breathing. The pool-water too had closed over as if it had frozen. Morgan forced herself under the arch.

'We must go,' she called to her son. She gave no reason why; she had none for herself – only that the monumental mother and father of this coming kingdom both wanted them to stay. All she knew was that Mordred was alive, not yet in the water. 'Oh, please now let's go . . .'

Mordred couldn't seem to tear himself away. But he wasn't a part of the larger stillness. '*Father* . . .' he shouted again, rolling the word around his mouth.

'With me . . .' Morgan told him across the great waiting space. 'I want you with me.' Aching because he didn't want to be with her, she bowed her head, supporting herself against one of the arch's columns.

Mordred scowled, a cheated child. But then he turned from the pool and trotted to her side. Without another word, Morgan pushed him in front of her and out to the top of the stairway.

He skipped down the steps ahead of her. Twice in her confusion she almost let herself fall. This fatigue was desperately familiar. A mighty post-coital drowsiness shot through with panic and pain.

This was how Arthur had always left her, sliding out of her before he came, twisting away as if suddenly he had been severed from some far larger over-arching tormentor. She saw yet again his black throbbing cross shake on his shoulder as he spent himself over her legs. Every time until the last time. Every time until she had held him fast.

The sublime city was silent – its streets bare, its waiting people nowhere. On the unbreachable walls the guards looked only outward. Even if Morgan had screamed, none would have turned. Deployed like gaming pieces on the night-sky's darkness, they could have been made of bone or horn.

Mordred looked to her for directions. Barely conscious on her feet, Morgan headed away from the gatehouse they had come through. A long well-lit avenue led to the lip of the hill, then swept down towards a point of exit in the interior curtain wall. They started to make for it.

The gates below, she saw, were closed. Mordred seemed to see it too. He ran in front of where she stood, smiling, springing from foot to foot, nodding, obviously wanting to go back. His man's mind had gone. He had so much life in him. Morgan had almost none. If she dropped now, she would roll down the slope until she crashed into the wall.

Then the pain came, and she clutched at her stomach. It felt flooded with fire. All she wanted was the dark. Her feet were taking her downward. The incline was steep; it made her calves scream. No houses here, just grass and night.

Her eyes were closed. She knew what would have been here in the king's old camp. *Arthur went . . . inside. He lived like the beast he had always been — in a pit dug under the court, where Bran's head was said to have been buried.*

She opened her eyes. To her right, built into the hill, lay a great disused grain-silo. Its doors were folded back; the wood black-damp and rotting. One last un-remade fragment of the new and better kingdom.

'Here,' she breathed to her son, nearly skidding on the mud at its mouth and then ducking in.

She couldn't think any further than this. The drop inside was sudden, but she kept her balance. Turning, she saw Mordred's little feet. She offered him her hand, but he never took it.

Spots of blood were speckling his toes. It was too late. Morgan couldn't haul herself out; she scarcely had the strength to keep up her arm. Fire blazed inside her.

'Come in,' she urged him, weeping. 'Come in to me . . .'

He stepped back, not forward. Briefly she saw his face. He was trying to smile, trying not to see the slashes at his shoulders. He shook his head at her, as if he understood.

As if he could drive all the evil away just by being so beautifully blameless.

Mordred turned and ran back up the slope. She heard only one more word. 'Father.'

And then, in the end, the child came back . . .

SEVENTEEN

It wasn't his blood. He wouldn't let it worry him. And the water would clear it away for ever. The water that had played with his knife; the water where he was meant to be.

His mother should have been coming too. But he knew she was tired. Time tired. Time didn't trouble him, though; he could keep running to and fro along this line for as long as anyone wanted. But that wasn't what he wanted. Just the water. To go in like the knife, and let the others clap.

He ran so fast in the dark. Over the crest and back down the avenue. Eating up the distance. Surging through the stillness. He could smell his own speed now. The cuts came, but no pain. Never any pain. He was safe in this city. Safe with the men up there on the walls. His mother should have known that. She should have known that he had to be about his father's business.

His legs were too short to take the steps at a dash. He wanted to leap three at a time. Instead he had to caterpillar his way up, bringing both feet together before he could kick out again. Stop-start, stop-start.

At the top his heart was louder. He took some breath and watched the blood. He liked the way it came: thinner from his mouth than from his chest. The air was thick up here. Time thick. Maybe the blood just came from the air. Like the drizzle before. Out of the air and into him, then out again turned red and runny. It spilled on the top step.

His ears drummed from the run and climb, but soon he was ready for more. Ready for the water. He dashed beneath the high, carved arch. Such a silly carving: men on horses going up, men on horses coming down; but right at the top was a king on a goat. A great big king on a baby bearded goat.

The pool was as he had left it. No mark where the knife had hit. The candles still burned there, though some had gone out. Doused by the drizzle.

He couldn't see the others. Maybe they had gone to be in holes like his mother? Maybe they too had been tired? Mordred hadn't liked her hole. Wet and dark and on and on – he'd seen how far it circled down. His mother didn't need to be in there; no one had to hide like that.

He pulled up short before a couch. There should have been people there – watching and waiting and ready to clap. The couches all made up a circular bench. The men on the walls should have sat there and waited. Those walls wouldn't fall. They should have looked inwards.

His clothes lay red on top of one couch, but he wouldn't need clothes when he went in the water. Even the knife's clothes had peeled off in there.

He ducked and crawled beneath the bench ring. Blood was in his eyes, but he wiped it away. This was where he had to be. He'd known it since waking; since stepping to the pool's edge when the others hadn't seen. And light had come up from the rippling water. Light that announced that his father was near. King from the water, the king from the water. This was his house, and the pool was his chamber. Down in the darkness his shadow shone bright.

So he had thrown him the knife as a present. Thrown him the knife just to show that he knew. This is my father's house, this is his chamber. This is the place where he wants me to be.

He stepped to the edge and again saw the shape there. Shimmering, welcoming, deep down below. Water once frightened him; not any longer. Water was good and it wasn't a hole. Here I am, Father. Here I am, take me . . . He took in more breath, crouched, then swung his arms low.

'No!'

The lady came forward, dragged out by her own sound. Out of the darkness she'd found by the wall. Opposite her the man came out slowly, his hands joined together as if they were fighting.

'No,' said the lady, her hand stretched towards him. Her face was now smiling, not sad like before. He reached back, she touched him, hot fingers with rings on.

He watched her hand closely. Their fingers were linked now. Up on the clothes-couch she raised him, still smiling. The blood drizzled down, but none went on her. She put him up high like a man on the wall, then took back her fingers and smiled at the water.

'Now,' she said. First 'No', then 'Now'.

The water didn't part at once. First it spilled up over the sides. Quietly, not angrily. Just lapping beneath the ring. Not touching Mordred, not reaching his feet.

Then the water opened. Not like water any more. Grey now, and streaked like the stone on the floor. It cracked and it splintered, not splashing, not wetting.

Mordred tried to clap but couldn't. Nor did the other two make any sound. No sound at all in the whole lovely city. No touch, no life, no time save for this.

But it didn't move forward in time's normal way. His father – the dark man – didn't rise up through the rubble: first head, then chest, then legs. He didn't come up as the knife had gone down. He came altogether, as if through a wall. A wall with no men on it. A wall from some old world. A wall he'd made fall just by being behind it.

Mordred smiled wide through the blood on his face. Cuts crossed his stomach. He dripped from his midriff. He wanted to clap but his hands wouldn't move. His smile used his strength up; he was all in his grin.

His father stood where the water had been: a great raised Round Table now. His clothes weren't wet, his hair was dry. For a moment he looked like a cross with his arms out. Then he was fully in line with himself, huge in his purple, a sword at his side. In one hand was a knife; the gift thrown by Mordred.

He stood proud and silent, and animal-sleek. A big man, a great man, broad-shouldered, tree-legged. Wherever his flesh showed, its colour was black – smothered in riots of hair never slashed. He looked like a bear there. Commanding, ferocious. His head rolled from side to side, sensing a new world – a world that belonged to him, solid and strong. He smiled and his teeth gleamed. Good, pitiless teeth. But his lips slipped back then, when his eye fell on Mordred.

'Father . . .' came to Mordred's throat, but it wouldn't push up higher. The word in its path now was 'king'. But Mordred couldn't say that. 'Father' was what he wanted. Then Mordred saw his other hand.

Two things in it. Both, at the start, were round; both, at the start, looked the same. One was golden, one creamy-whiter. Bands, hoops, big rings – both as big as Mordred's neck. His father held them loosely, like quoits he might then throw. The gold band had a head in it: open-mouthed, fanged, swallowing its tail. The whiter band had no head; it wasn't even round any more. Mordred thought it looked like rope.

His eyes were on Mordred. He was coming towards him. He didn't smile, his teeth were concealed. From closer his hair looked like iron: dazzle-black with spits of white. His eyes were so much higher than Mordred's. The knife in his hand was close to the top of Mordred's head. The blade had blood on it. Not Mordred's blood. Just the blood coming out of him. Through him.

Mordred smiled at his father's great flat stomach. He was vast, a wall himself. He had a smell, too. Spicy. Stirring. Hot like Mordred's mother's.

The head on the gold band was that of a dragon. Mordred liked it; he wanted to stroke it, but he had too much blood on him. The whiter band hung soft. Mordred knew it: from the knife's handle. Swimming away like a snake; but now it was dead. Or maybe just resting.

'Show him,' came the lady's voice. Mordred could hear that she was smiling. The lady who had kept him from the water, so grey in her gown that she could have been made from smoke. 'Show your father where your mother is.'

Mordred looked up. He needed to look at the face above, but all he could see was the great spill of beard. He wanted to see his father's eyes, to read there what *he* wanted.

'Now,' said the man and the lady together. Their voices rang everywhere. They were all inside the shell of it, even his father. 'Show him . . .'

And Mordred turned, jumped down and ran.

The floor was warm, the steps outside were hotter. Mordred descended without looking back – his father behind him with knife, band and rope. His father: the king who had looked like a cross.

The city seemed to lie in wait, holding its breath for what came next.

'Mother!' Mordred shrieked in mid-skip, while still too far away for her to hear. 'We're coming! . . .'

His father had to be with her. Father and mother together; not hiding. But still Mordred didn't look back. He could have seen his father's face now; he could have looked in his eyes. But he didn't. He just led him on, on to the end.

The slope began. Mordred saw the hole; he pointed and yelled. His legs gave way, he hit the ground on his chest and chin. The pain was sharp but quickly gone. He tried to cry and waved his arms; he wasn't the same, he'd softened all over. Unable to stand, unable to speak . . .

A hand closed on his back, then slid round to his front. A big hand, warm and hardened. Even as it lifted him, he softened and shrank again. Pushed against the purple cloth, he closed his eyes and smelt the spice.

King from the water . . . The king from the water . . . He thought he must be sleeping. The motion wasn't his now. Going down, from deep to deep. The hand held him lightly. Hand with a knife in it. Baby and blade.

He opened his eyes: they were going inside. Into the earth again. Hole in the hill. A sound like a wall rose to wrap him around.

Morgan screamed, too deep in his shadow to have any thoughts.

There were no steps now to take her higher. She curled against the silo's wall, crushing the husks with the weight of her pain. She bit on her wrist like a creature deranged. Licked at the wall as if that might make her safe.

His father said nothing. His father was touching him.

Pressing his belly down there in the dark. The snake seemed to circle him, white and then red-blue. Not dead now, not resting. Twisting and rearing, it bit on his belly flesh, started to suck.

She wouldn't turn, she wouldn't see him, as his breath mixed with her own. The heat shot through her in the silence. Then a sound: an infant's whimper.

He dragged back her arm and thrust on the armlet. Morgan screamed; mouthed 'queen' straight after, as if she'd never been deposed.

He didn't turn her, wrenched her rump up, ripped her gown and fed it in. Not himself though. Screaming, screaming. Not him down there. His hand at her throat; the touch of a blade. And down below: like a single, twisting finger, deeper, deeper. Not him but the cord. And then she felt the baby's cold, mucous pressure. Biting her vagina because still it was too old.

The scream wasn't his. He liked the snake in him.

He curled round the snake head; he had to be smaller. His father pushed harder. The darkness grew larger. He went through the wall.

The blade was sharp below her ear, urging her over. She rolled and he was on her, hoisting up her legs and going in after their child.

Everything she needed. Here in the deepest dark where nothing ever changed. He moved like a great tired beast inside her, vying with the child, sweeping from side to side, giving nothing, aiming only to take: to suck back his own juices. Time touched Morgan nowhere. She was outside everything.

And then, between blinks, she met his eye with hers.

At once the child climbed higher, clinging to itself, somersaulting smaller. Mordred: my son. Morgan thrilled to feel it. She had power, and at last she was using it truly, because of her love for Mordred, because he had given it meaning.

The child was on the steps again, outdistancing the shadow, just for as long as he had to. Arthur racked up after, scorching with his fire, but the waters kept the baby safe.

The steps ran up to the surface of this slope, soared past the wall with its unseeing sentries, on to where the morning waited. And Mordred briefly left her, flat-bellied again, to climb them on his own.

Arthur, oblivious, dropped the knife and gripped her hard. Already he was twisting away. He lost his hold and shivered, believing he'd now won the last war of all.

But then, in the end, the child came back down.

To the Fay.

Morgan slept soundly until she heard the shouts above. Triumphal cries. Roars of acclamation. A kingdom's stampede up the slope to its king.

Dawn flowed golden into her abyss. She uncurled in her corner and ran her fingers over the knife's hilt. She was pleased that he had left it; left her with so much: all she would be needing.

There was no pain. Barely any shame. He had drawn down her dress before slinking away. Back up to where he now belonged.

Smiling, scooping up the knife, she stood. The armlet slid from her wrist, dropped to the earth floor and rolled down deeper into the dark: the beast had gone back to its bottomless pit. Morgan's hand strayed to her stomach. The touch of her fingers was echoed inside. Everything . . .

Few saw her hoist herself out of her hell mouth. She was quick. She felt limber — a whole age younger than yesterday. Everyone was surging upward: an army of the fortunate reborn.

They had no reason to pause. Their king was waiting to bring them into his future. Their animal king, an emperor now in the making, re-conceived by new stories. Such scintillating stories.

Morgan watched them flood by — a ready, handsome people.

She pulled back her hair and knotted it up. The gates below were open for the inrush. She made for them in no great haste. The tide was all against her. Some pairs of eyes almost met hers in passing, but she knew she wasn't recognized. Not that morning. Later, some of them might remember that they had seen her go: the Fay who was moving in the opposite direction. Later, new levy men would be sent to track her down. By then she would be far away. By then she would have started to spin a story of her own — not Guenever's, not Merlin's, more sombre than their dreams of empire.

This time it was going to be different — for Arthur's people, for herself; most of all for Mordred.

This time, without question, he would be her son. Hers alone. This time there would be no unnecessary sacrifice. He would stay with her, and grow in their own golden darkness beyond these poorly founded walls. And when he came back he would come in such blood.

At the gatehouse the incomers, mostly elderly now, parted to let her through. Morgan passed out of Camelot and headed for the north of the kingdom of Logres.

THE MORDRED CYCLE continues in
The Knight's Vengeance . . .

THE KING'S EVIL

A Mordred Cycle Novel

Haydn Middleton

A seed sown in darkness will surely blossom in an evil way . . .

Mordred, the tainted innocent, comes of age in a remote corner of the land of Arthur. Always a law unto himself, he is troubled by the visits of the cryptic 'strays'. Challenging him, they offer the keys not only to Arthur's kingdom, but also to a darker, uncharted realm within Mordred himself. Now at last he must confront the mystery of his birth and embark on a cyclical quest, leading him to both destiny and nemesis . . .

'Breathes life into a classic story . . . a fine piece of fantasy writing with a powerful, shocking ending'
Don't Tell It

'Proof that the Arthurian characters are still capable of sustaining multiple interpretations'
Time Out

Warner
0 7515 1299 0

THE KNIGHT'S VENGEANCE

A Mordred Cycle Novel

Haydn Middleton

A seed sown in darkness will surely blossom in an evil way . . .

The Great Remaking is complete. King Arthur has led his people from ruined Albion into the promised land of Logres. But within a year – for reasons that no one is able to fathom – he is leading his armies back to war.

His relentless overseas campaigns last for a decade. In his absence Logres – maybe the truer battleground all along – undergoes subtle but profound changes. Arthur returns to a people who seem almost oblivious to Camelot's ruling elite. Their allegiance has turned instead to a strange cult that is both newer and far more ancient than any conventional monarchy.

Clouds gather on the northern horizon. Man-shaped clouds that tell stories of their own. Meanwhile a woman at the island-kingdom's edge nurtures a boy through to adulthood. Inexorably, now, he heads towards King Arthur's court . . .

A Little, Brown Hardback
0 316 91369 3

| ☐ The King's Evil | Haydn Middleton | £5.99 |
| ☐ The Knight's Vengeance | Haydn Middleton | £16.99 |

Warner Books now offers an exciting range of quality titles by both established and new authors. All of the books in this series are available from:

Little, Brown and Company (UK),
P.O. Box 11,
Falmouth,
Cornwall TR10 9EN.
Telephone No: 01326 372400
Fax No: 01326 317444
E-mail: books@barni.avel.co.uk

Payments can be made as follows: cheque, postal order (payable to Little, Brown and Company) or by credit cards, Visa/Access. Do not send cash or currency. UK customers and B.F.P.O. please allow £1.00 for postage and packing for the first book, plus 50p for the second book, plus 30p for each additional book up to a maximum charge of £3.00 (7 books plus).

Overseas customers including Ireland, please allow £2.00 for the first book plus £1.00 for the second book, plus 50p for each additional book.

NAME (Block Letters) ....

....

ADDRESS ....

....

....

☐ I enclose my remittance for ....

☐ I wish to pay by Access/Visa Card

Number | | | | | | | | | | | | | | | | | | |

Card Expiry Date | | | | |